The Assassin,
The Grey Man
And
The Surgeon

By D C Stansfield

The Assassin, The Grey Man and The Surgeon series:

Book 1: The Assassin, The Grey Man and The Surgeon

Book 2: To Kill a Grey Man

Book 3: A Wicked Profit

Book 4: The Russians and the Beast

Other books by D C Stansfield:

Tom Revilo

An Assassin For The New Templars

A One Sided Game

A Griffin A Murder and A Mason

Never Run, Never Hide

Chapter 1

It was a stinking night. The rain pelted down on the windscreen causing visibility to be almost zero. Jon did not like this at all. He had only just passed his driving test and tonight as he peered through the mist, he decided that he hated the rain and he hated the small roads and he hated the countryside. As far as he was concerned trying to find the tiny village in deepest Sussex was impossible. He had stopped twice to get directions before finally with relief found the main street, what there was of it, and turned into the courtyard of a shabby pub, an old coaching inn that had definitely seen better days.

Through the dark and rain swept heavy glass of the bay window, he could just see the barman pulling a pint under a bright bare neon bulb. Waiting for a break in the rain, he ran for the porch. Clicking the Audi's key fob to lock the car doors Jon shook himself dry and walked into the pub. The smell of stale beer washed over him and he took a seat at the filthy old bar on a stool with a red plastic, split seat with the foam poking through. Dirty stained glasses hung from hooks behind the counter and the bare floor hadn't been swept for a long time. The walls were coarse plaster and yellowed with age and smoke, a few moth eaten old pictures hung tiredly here and there.

The youngish, scruffy barman dressed in old jeans and a dirty blue T-shirt that had seen better days, gave him a surly look as he ordered a beer. He felt completely out of place. Nineteen years old, styled haircut, polished black leather shoes and wearing a heavy black overcoat and blue and yellow university scarf Jon looked what he was, a middle class student in a working class pub. An alien from a different planet could not have looked more out of place. To the left of him sat an old drunk in his 70's huddled over his glass, wearing a stained raincoat which once must have once been beige, muttering inanities to himself. To the right at the end of the bar were two tattooed thugs, complete with cropped haircuts and earrings, ripped T-shirts and boots. The smaller one had a set of greasy overalls pushed off his shoulders with the arms tied round his waist. In the middle of them was a young girl, he guessed no more than 16. She was crying softly, too much makeup, a short skirt and tight top trying to look older then her years. "I need to go home. My dad will be waiting" she cried. The bigger of the thugs said, "Nah, let me finish this and we can go back to my place" and he leered at his smaller mate. Jon was careful not to catch either's eye.

The only other customer was in the corner of the room, an old man sitting at a beer stained table, Jon guessed sixty-something, reading a much used, old paperback, he had thinning salt and pepper coloured, lanky greasy hair, balding at the crown, with a flushed drink-filled unshaven face, had a large build with a beer gut barely kept in place by a scruffy, stained checked shirt and old trousers over scuffed shoes. 'He's not here,' Jon thought and settled in. 'I will give him an hour and then phone home for instructions'.

Jon sat quietly full of sadness. He had received the bad news about his mother two days ago during a break in lessons, driven to the house as quickly as he could and then waited for his father to come home.

He thought back over the day. It had been a tough one. Jon had watched his father perform as friends and relatives filed through the front room offering condolences and advice in the sprawling 1930's house they called home. It was in a quiet street in the heart of suburbia where everyone mowed their lawn and washed their cars on a Sunday. The quietness of the surroundings added to the sombre aspect of the day's events.

At all times during the day his father retained the quiet dignity that was so part of his character. It was only towards the end, in the late afternoon, when they had all drifted away that Jon saw any emotion. His dad looked old, tired and drawn, pacing restlessly up and down the carpet in the dining room, deep in thought obviously wrestling with some problem or other.

Finally his father stopped pacing as he came to a decision. Then he said, "Jon have you ever heard this? '*I will pursue my enemies and overtake them; Nor will I turn again until they are consumed; I will smite them through that they shall not be able to rise; they shall fall under my feet*' (Psalms 18, verses 38 and 39)

"No," said Jon.

"It is the way I feel," said his father. He sat down opposite his son and looked him in the eye. "I am so sorry about what happened," he continued. "If I were here, maybe I could have stopped it."

Jon shook his head. "And maybe not," he said.

His father went on. "There is a lot you don't know about me. There's a lot I had put behind me, but I cannot stand by and let what has happened pass without reacting. I plan to go on a course of action which will be violent and dangerous and I cannot leave you behind. I need your help. You will be treading a path I promised your mother I would keep you away from. You are ill equipped for this but for me it is the only way. Are you with me?"

Jon looked his father in the eyes. He loved the little man and without hesitation said, "Always."

"Good. This is your first job." He took a pen and paper from a side drawer and wrote down two addresses. "I need you to go to this pub first, find a man I know and deliver him to the second address where I will be waiting."

"What is his name?" asked Jon.

"I have always called him Surge but I don't know what he goes by now," said his father. "He will probably be using a different name from that one. He is not a man who wants to be found. Look for a big man. He's in his fifties now but probably looks younger. He always sits alone. If possible sitting well back from the main area with views of all exits, reading a book and dressed down, trying to blend in, which he normally fails to achieve. He will look fit, of military bearing, hair cut short, trousers with razor edges and parade room shoes. There is something about him that makes him stand out amongst other men. You will know what I mean when you see him. Tell him that Collins sent you. He will say that he is not the person I knew. Tell him he gave his word and his word is iron. Trust me, he will come. He will not let you drive directly to this address but will play some games. Do exactly what he says. Oh, and Jon, Surge attracts trouble like a magnet. Tread carefully around him. He is a very dangerous, violent man."

Back in the pub, Jon focussed on the present. The minutes ticked by, the girl became more upset and the drunk louder in his murmuring. The old man in the corner finished his pint and slowly rose to come to the bar staggering a little, obviously worse for wear. He did not look at the barman, just placed his glass down and as the barman filled it, paid the exact amount in small coins from a brown rectangular folding purse. The girl started to cry again pleading with the men to let her go, but the smaller thug put his arm round her and held her close.

As the old man turned his foot caught against a stool and he lurched forward. The beer from his pint splashed over the bigger thug who turned and smashed a punch full into the older man's face. He skidded back hitting the wall hard and slid down. The thug moved forward standing over him menacingly. "Come on. Get up you old bastard!" he shouted, red faced with rage, spittle and beer running from his chin. The old man hardly looked at the thug. He just stared at the barman who behind the thugs back, stretched out his arm and pointed a finger at him, so he lay there blood running from his split lip, a blank expression on his face with the thug glaring down at him. Before the attack could be followed up the smaller thug shouted "Stop!" In the confusion, the girl had twisted from his grip and run out the back. Both thugs raced after her.

The old man picked himself up, wiped the blood from his face with a neatly folded handkerchief which he took from his trouser pocket, took what was left of his pint back to his seat, sat down and started reading his book again as if nothing had happened.

"What's his story?" Jon asked the barman.

"Fucking troublemaker!" he said. "Comes in here every night with a different book in all sorts of weird languages - German, French, Russian you name it, sits in the corner and drinks till he has had enough or I kick him out. Never says a word to anyone, but trouble just comes to him like you would not believe. He's banned from every pub in the village for fighting. We are the last pub. If I ban him, he has nowhere to go"

Jon felt sorry for the old man and on impulse bought him another beer and wandered over to him just as the thugs came back without the girl, moaning and cursing. "You spilt your pint." Jon said, putting the new pint in front of the old man. The man looked up. He had a tired, dishevelled look about him. "Thanks," he muttered, but as Jon pulled a seat out and sat down the old man said shortly "I like to drink alone". He had a quiet voice with no trace of a regional accent. Jon remained seated and the atmosphere between them grew tense. The man was obviously unhappy and said "If you want the table....." and half rose looking at Jon directly in the eyes. It was a jolt - bright blue eyes that looked directly into Jon's soul. The hair on the back of Jon's neck stiffened. He could not believe it. Could this be the man his dad had sent him for? The military man? Surely not. But he decided to take a chance and leant across the table and whispered, "Collins sent me." He watched the colour drain from the old man's face. After a few seconds he said, "Tell him you could not find me."

"He said you would say that," replied Jon smiling.

Starting to raise his voice and spitting out the words the old man said, "Tell him I cannot even handle a pub fight. I am not the man he knew."

"He also told me that you promised and your word is iron," said Jon.

The man paused, struggling for an answer that would not come. He looked at the floor for a few seconds, straightened and said, "When?"

"Now," said Jon and stood up. The old man reluctantly got to his feet. As they walked past the thugs the larger one scowled and said, "Don't you ever fucking show your face in here again granddad or I will cut it off!" The old man didn't look at him just put his head down and kept on walking.

Once outside they stood in the porch gathering themselves together before stepping into the rain. The old man patted his pockets

"I forgot my book. Give me a second," he said.

"Is that wise?" asked Jon.

The old man shrugged, "It's a good book," he replied and turned back.

As he went through the bar door a change came over him. His face set and if anyone was watching they would see his body came alive with tension but no one was looking . The big thug stepped in front of him blocking his passage, about to say something clever as the first punch came out of the blue surprising the thug entirely. A chopping left just below the ear, the punch so sharp and crisp it immediately knocked him out and he stood there wavering, unconscious his eyes rolling back in his head as if a light had been switched off. Before his body realised he was unconscious and started to collapse the old man stepped carefully to the right and struck powerfully and deliberately with two right hand punches. The first ended with a click as the thug's jaw dislocated, the second more powerful strike gave off a crunching sound as it broke the cheekbone. Both punches were delivered so quickly that they landed as the thug was halfway to the floor and were vicious and completely unnecessary . The attack was executed with no fanfare, quiet, sharp and professional that spoke of long practice. The other thug took one step forward to get involved and then thought better of it disappearing out the back door as if he was on fire. The barman, shocked, also started to step forward. The old man straightened, raised his arm and pointed his finger. A copy of the barman's reaction earlier and without looking at him said "Not one word. Not one fucking word."

Surge joined Jon on the porch a second later, faced flushed. "Have you got it?" asked Jon. "Yeah" said the man patting his pocket, "No problem" and they ran together through the rain to the car.

Inside the car Jon managed a sideways look at his passenger. Maybe not sixty he thought but no spring chicken. He smelt of beer and slightly of body odour.

"What shall I call you?" said Jon. "My dad was not that specific, just described you to me."

"Your dad?" the man said, "I thought I could see him in you. Call me Surge."

"Is that your real name?" asked Jon.

"No just one that's sort of stuck. Where are we going?"

"London," replied Jon as he gunned the car through the wet, black lanes. The man called Surge leant back in his seat and promptly fell asleep.

Jon thought, "Who the hell is this? Has dad gone mad?"

Chapter 2

It was later in that soaking wet evening with black clouds high overhead and a chill in the air that The Grey Man found his piece of the shadows. He stood very still backed into a doorway. A sad, small man in dull clothes looking for all the world like one of humanity's lost people, the kind you ignore rather than have to spend a second interacting with. If you looked up the word non-descript in the dictionary it would have his name against it. He was studying a flat above a butchers' shop where the meeting would take place it looked ordinary like so many others along the row. It was a normal London high street. People bustled in and out of the few shops ignoring him completely. He stood and watched as the people hurried by. As far as they were concerned he was not there - it was a talent he had always had since he was a young boy. The child of a drunken mother and a violent father who, when not kicking the dog around, kicked him. He had learnt from a very early age whether it was safe to go home. He would call out 'hello' and the reply indicated whether he could come in or it was best to leave. At a young age he developed a talent for sensing the mood and learned when and how to disappear. To this day the beatings and the cursing he received so many decades ago still occupied his dreams.

At twelve years old social services finally caught up and he was taken to a care institution in the back streets of London. He thought it was bad at home but this was infinitely worse. This was where he really learnt about violence and evil and child rape and how to endure a total lack of care, to understand the indifference that somehow was much more evil then hate. For a quiet introspective boy, this was hell, but he endured it and in his own way learned to fight back, to survive. He refined his skill in sensing mood, learned how to watch and how to react, learned how to be inoffensive and how and when to be strong but mainly the greatest talent he learnt was how to become invisible. He developed a greyness, an ability to be part of the furniture, outwardly calm but internally his antenna tuned to every noise, facial expression and body language. He became so good at it that at age thirteen he went walkabout. He just woke up one day, packed a few things and walked out. Nobody noticed for three days then the alarm went off. Even an institution like this could not lose a boy. They found him six months later in a small croft in Scotland, half starved and worn out. He had finally trusted an old widow woman who had given him food and a bed before turning him into the police who bought him back to purgatory. She thought she was doing him a good turn. That was the last time he had ever trusted anyone.

His great break came when he was 16. He travelled on the tube into London to a small branch of the Civil Service where he worked as a lowly clerk, a job the care home had found for him. He kept to himself as usual, just communicating enough not to appear strange, so any oddness, quirk or abnormality that might make him interesting was definitely out liking the cloak of invisibility this gave him. He quietly went about his business, blending into the background, trying to act normal and perhaps even a bit boring, always polite but distant, not making any friends or having any communication with his fellow workers outside of work.

For six months he worked moderately hard at a nothing job. At the bottom of the ladder he had no idea what the department did and no real interest in the business types who popped in and out at irregular times. Something to do with foreign policy he thought. Unbeknown to him however he had been spotted by an expert, someone who looked for the quiet, invisible types. In the world that person worked in it was almost a prerequisite and so he set the boy a simple trap.

The Grey Man wasn't interested in promotion but a job had come up overseas and he quite fancied travelling. He was interviewed and set an aptitude test which was difficult but somehow, even with his limited background, managed to struggle through it. His schooling had been intermittent and poor but afterwards unbelievably felt he had done well. Unusually for him, a person who tried to stay uncaring about such matters, became overcome with curiosity and on impulse went about quietly finding out where the results were.

He had watched his manager open the office safe many times. It was quite often left unlocked and was obviously not that secure. Just for the fun of it The Grey Man had memorised the combination and on a quiet Wednesday afternoon following the exam he had slipped into the manager's office, opened the safe and sat at the desk looking at the results.

On cue the door burst open and he was caught red handed. They had trapped him perfectly. There was some money in the safe and the Manager threatened to report him to the police. They left him to stew for a while in the office alone, before another quiet small man came in and offered him a deal, all charges would be dropped if he would agree to work for them. There was, as expected, no real option.

The next few years were bliss for The Grey Man. After signing the Official Secrets Act he was told he was now working for the Secret Service and they trained him in all manner of covert operations. At first they thought he might be of use as a spy, a field operative, but disappointingly he was not up to standard as he lacked the social skills, the warmth necessary to con his way into people's lives, gain their trust and then lie and betray.

After some months of watching and experimenting they finally found out what he could do, which to the surprise of everybody he did so well that over the years he surpassed all others, including his instructors.

On the face of it, it was a simple skill. He could watch without getting noticed. He could stand in the most conspicuous place and people would pass him by without noticing him. He could meet people and when they were asked afterwards what he looked like they could not point out one distinguishing mark or pick him out from a line up. It was unique and impossible and fascinating. Add that to a fantastic memory and he slowly became The Grey Man, the information gatherer.

As the years passed, because he had no distractions, no partners, no family, no friends, no one close enough to take up his time, he was able to add other skills – electronics, computers, languages, developing his mind in many areas, studying everything he needed to become The Grey Man. Within a few years he had started to work all over the world memorising faces, times, dates and places. His capacity for gathering information was staggering and was much in demand. He managed to acquire many skills through an almost religious devotion to his craft becoming unquestionably the best. It had been a long, hard but deeply absorbing life which he had spent alone almost in complete isolation, an island of one. But he knew, as much as he hated to mix with people, that there was still some spark of humanity left in him. Some longing for what might have been had he had a normal upbringing.

A few years before, he set himself a test and bought a small cottage in the wilds of the Shetland Isles, far away from civilisation, and decided to cut himself off once and for all, from humanity, the rat race and people. Sever all human contact. He lasted four months and six days before he gave it up, sitting on the moors completely alone he felt he was sitting there waiting to die and wondered then if that was OK, perhaps he should die. What really did he have to live for? But somehow knew he was not ready yet, for some inexplicable reason The Grey Man needed people, at least at the edge of his life, and so gave up the cottage going back to the only thing he really knew, his watching. Perhaps he thought, that's why, when Collins approached him he had agreed to the deal.

The Grey Man stood as he had stood for the past three hours. He neither acknowledged the cold or recognised the stiffening of his aging body, the twinge of rheumatism in his ankle or the pain in his hip. Standing perfectly still, to him, was everything. People saw motion, they responded to movement. Stillness gave him invisibility, just one of the many tools developed over lifetime.

He wondered again over and over why he was standing there, what the real reason was that he put himself through the agony why he kept watching hour after hour. As was his way, he ran through his routine. He had memorised every car in detail, registration plate, colour and marks, wheel trims, stickers, drivers and types of passenger that had driven by. He could recall them at will. He knew he would remember in detail everyone who had walked past even if they came back in disguise. He could tell them by their walk or the way their body moved. He looked for patterns in passers-by, anyone who was hanging around or pretending to read a paper or eat some food or just plain out of place. He, in short, went through all the tricks of the surveillance game to ensure the meeting was clean.

His routine was the ultimate 'Kim's Game' and he was the best. He could review everything he had seen at will and then, when he knew it was of no use, could wipe it from his memory. So he stood and watched and waited.

He had no need to move from where he was to keep the flat under surveillance. Any operative worth their salt would circle the building at least once on a recce and The Grey Man would spot them.

The call that had come from Collins two days ago had arrived through a convoluted route that he had agreed with him some time ago. There could be no one sent for him like there had been for Surge, as who could find The Grey Man? There had just been a series of emails through third parties and finally a coded telephone number.

He had been briefed by Collins on what had happened and had already started looking into the matter. Feeding Collins back some significant information he wondered what Collins would do - acting on intel was different from just receiving it.

Why he had set this communication route up and why he had come to stand in this doorway was a mystery to him. The years of abuse and isolation had, he thought, burnt out all form of friendship or trust. Intimacy of any form was an anathema to him and neither sex was of any interest physically. He was a man alone looking in on the world, or so he thought, so why was he now standing in the middle of a high street, cold and wet scanning for enemies?

The deal Collins had offered him those years ago was a simple one. He assumed Surge had the same offer. There were a number of people in the great game who were getting long in the tooth, from hard men to shooters, counter espionage to field agents and watchers. Many were becoming too old to continue doing what they did, either they were burnt out or were compromised or forcibly retired.

These people all had a past with unfinished business and Collins argued that as they got older they could become vulnerable. Certainly the agencies they worked for would not be interested, in fact, would disown them completely. There was no retirement help for these types, just a push into the cold with the Official Secrets Act carved into your soul.

The deal offered was to form an unofficial brotherhood between only professional long term operatives such as himself. If any of them got into trouble they would first try to deal with it on their own, or sell up and move on. Only if all else failed only as a last resort they could call on their colleagues in the brotherhood to come and help. It sounded simple and in a tough world, prudent. This was the first time he had thought about it since.

The truth was that in this case Collins was in no danger at all. In fact Collins, if he was a different man, could walk away. But The Grey Man thought he would not. It was a matter of honour and revenge, all to do with family and background and tradition. The Grey Man struggled with these concepts. He had little to do with any of these issues. Maybe, he thought, that's why he was there to find out, still gathering information. And the rain started to pour down again and he stood and watched.

The man they called Collins, a name that had just stuck from all the aliases he had used in the past, was pacing up and down the small, neat apartment above the butcher's shop. Furnished like all safe houses, in a featureless style with cheap, serviceable furniture and a doctor's waiting room type atmosphere. Occasionally he looked out the window and then started pacing again. Finally he stopped in front of a full sized mirror hung on the back of the door and stared at his reflection. He looked exactly the way he wanted to look. Every second of his sixty five years was written on his face and he wore his nationality like a badge, from the black shirt to the grey cardigan, black trousers and comfortable shoes. He looked like a Jewish, corner shop store keeper which was exactly what he was now. OK, technically he owned a shop which technically had been his wife's and his main business was an import/export plus consultancy on a few matters best not discussed, but he was still 'a little old Jewish shopkeeper'.

He liked the way he looked, as if life was taking him back in a full circle to his birthplace and religion. He stared hard at the reflection trying to find the younger man, the one who had stood on the Golam Heights with the AK47 over his shoulder and shouted defiance at the world. The man who had killed with gun and knife and hand to hand combat, who had been born into fire and hate, the man who once upon a time could stand toe-to-toe with anyone living and come out victorious. That man was long gone now. Just a storekeeper looked back. What then of the man that came after the soldier, the assassin killing in the dark anywhere in the world, accurate with any gun, who could take out a target from over a mile away, a man who killed with no remorse before disappearing, who hunted and killed the most deadly terrorists and murderers? He peered into the mirror looking hard. There was no sign of him, just the little, Jewish shopkeeper tired, worn out and old kept staring back at him.

He finally turned his mind to his dead wife and the emotions started to come to the surface. His blood started to course through his body as he let his anger grow. He thought, let the world see what they wanted to, he was the sum of everything that had gone before and he knew there was more than a spark left of the old him. They had touched his family and would rue that day. He was not interested in justice, only revenge and gradually as he looked harder, the eyes in the mirror changed and he saw what he wanted to see - not the shopkeeper, he faded away, but a man of evil looked back, a man devoid of pity or mercy or forgiveness. A man who dealt in death.

He stepped away from the mirror now satisfied and thought again about what he had done. The process he had put in place with The Grey Man and the mission he had sent Jon on. The Grey Man was probably as old as he was, maybe older. Would he be what he was? Could you still be the best when your body no longer functioned as it should? Would his mind be as sharp and his almost magical abilities still be there?

He hadn't seen Surge for over 5 years, just before Surge had got into his trouble and ended up in the hospital and then left the Service. At that time he was the most dangerous man he had ever known and his exploits were legendary. Collins had a lifetime of mixing with violent men, but none was like Surge. Even his name was an 'in' joke - Surge was short for The Surgeon, as it was rumoured each time he hit someone he cut them. A hard man. What would he be like now? He must be fifty at least. How long can you be a hard man before younger men show you up with the embarrassment of age? When your speed and strength give out, what are you then?

But Collins had no choice and no one else to turn to. Would it be enough and would they agree? He walked again to the window and looked out. He knew if The Grey Man was there he would not see him so decided instead to go down and unlock the back door. The Grey Man did not need the help but would appreciate the gesture. Then for the fifth time he adjusted the chairs minutely. Neither of his guests liked to sit in the open and both would want views of the entrance and exit without being close to the windows. Tradecraft never goes away.

Jon and Surge arrived first. Jon clattered up the stairs and embraced his father. Collins stepped back and examined his son. A good looking, tall well formed 19 year old dressed in his university style uniform, jeans and sweat shirt with coat and long university scarf, straight black hair swept back from his eyes and a pleasing open face. He had lived a life of privilege in a safe normal world. Collins wondered how he would take to the new one he was going to be pushed into. University life was no training ground for violence, intrigue and death.

Surge lumbered up the stairs and shook Collins hand. Collins tried not to look shocked as he took in the florid, drink-hardened face and saw the years of weight. He looked fat and tired but most of all, he looked old. Collins knew at once he had made a huge mistake. This was not the professional man who had spent his whole life training to be an awesome fighting machine. He could smell the beer and lack of care. How could he have fallen so far he thought?

Surge took a seat and they waited until The Grey Man appeared at the door some fifteen minutes later. "Anyone following?" asked Collins but The Grey Man shook his head then gave a nod at Surge and Jon before sitting down. At least he had not changed. Still a dapper little man, wearing, as always to meetings, a grey three piece suit, smart but not too smart, thought Collins smiling. It did not do to stand out.

Collins started to pace up and down. "Thank you for coming," he began. "I hoped you would. I need your help. Let me state up front that the course of action I am about to embark on, any sane man would walk away from. It is not me under attack. I am attacking someone else. For me it is a matter of duty and honour - something I am committed to. I realise this is outside the deal we agreed and I would understand if you do not want to get involved, but as you know, sometimes in life you have to make a stand and that time for me is now."

"There is a gang of villains who have started to target ethnic businessmen," he continued. "Not the big guys but the small entrepreneurs, shop keepers and restaurateurs. Mainly hardworking family operations, the kind that are first generation immigrants unsure of their place in English society, the kind that dislike going to the police or causing any kind of disruption which might find them investigated by the UK government. Many are used to paying some kind of protection money to someone either here or where they come from."

"Nothing new in that," interrupted Surge.

"No," Collins replied. "But this team have a subtle twist. The price for protection starts off small then week by week gets bigger until the poor guy cannot possibly pay. He is then offered an out, a way to ease the burden. All he has to do is to bring in a small parcel from his mother country every now and then. Almost all of these people have ties with their homeland. They all buy local products which you cannot get here which appeal to them or their customers. The deal they are offered is to occasionally receive a random parcel alongside their legitimate one, with no questions asked. The result is either a small reward to the compliant ones or a significant reduction in the weekly protection bill. What, of course, is in the parcel and unknown to the receiver, is heroin."

"These parcels must be quite small," said The Grey Man. "And therefore surely on their own would not be worth anyone's while."

"True," said Collins. "But what if this was part of a growing network, a pyramid of receivers? Have you any idea how many ethnic businessmen there are in London and how many parcels get delivered each week? I phoned around some colleagues in this neighbourhood. Many of them have been targeted already and are involved. If you multiply that coverage across London, the results are shocking. I estimate that these villains are currently receiving at least one hundred and fifty parcels plus per week, something like 25lbs of heroin. Normally this junk would go through at least five different hands, each cutting the product before arriving in London. But what is significant about these parcels is the product is pure, straight from the fields which can be cut to give at least ten times the volume in street drugs, so at least 250lbs of saleable shit per month. That's a lot of little bags."

"The profit must be phenomenal and virtually no risk. Anything going wrong, the storekeeper gets in trouble not the villains and even then only individual small amounts would be seized, just enough to play down a first offence. The storekeeper would probably walk. All of which makes the deal quite attractive to the victims especially when you are losing your livelihood due to extortion."

"How come Customs have not caught them?" asked Surge.

"Simple," replied Collins. "Some of these businessmen have been importing for years completely legitimately. They have been checked and rechecked and nothing ever shows up so they become background noise. Custom officials do not have the resources nor are they looking for established importers; they are looking for new importers, differences in practice and large volumes. Here, there is just routine. Each shopkeeper only receives small amounts at random along with their normal deliveries and are completely independent of each other so there is no pattern. Customs want big fish with big networks. Who would believe that a significant proportion of small ethnic companies in London were involved in smuggling? Impossible but true. The leaders are clever. They limit each shopkeeper to one small parcel every now and again, constantly changing the path to the UK. For Customs to open the right parcel on the right day the odds are very small."

"I have some questions," said Surge. "Why have you not gone to the police and blown the whistle and failing that why do you even care? Why have you not just sold up and walked away if they are targeting you?"

"I can answer your questions with this," said Collins and he nodded at Jon who walked over to the TV and pushed a button. What appeared on the screen was a grainy film of CCTV from a security camera in what looked like a small corner shop filming from a high place behind the counter. They could see the door opening and customers coming in and out and occasionally the back of the head of a short, round, middle aged woman who was serving. Suddenly, in burst a man wearing a hooded sweater. The hood was pulled down to conceal his face. He said something to the woman, pulled out a hand gun and shot her twice in the head, then pocketed the gun and walked out. The whole scene took under ten seconds.

There was a silence in the room and Jon shut the TV down. "That," said Collins quietly "was my wife." The room remained silent as Collins continued. "I had been travelling for a couple of weeks and my wife was running her corner shop business as normal. As far as I can ascertain a man came in a few days before this incident and went through the protection spiel. My wife kicked him out and told him she was calling the police. She did not want to worry me so did not mention it when I phoned home. The next thing I knew was Jon calling me telling me she was dead. That was two days ago."

Very quietly The Grey Man said, "What do you need?"

"I want to break this organisation and find the men at the top and once I do, they are dead. To paraphrase an old proverb, *Against the avenging of a wife and mother's death the devil himself is powerless."*

Once again there was silence. Finally it was broken by The Grey Man.

"OK," he said, "I can find them and give you all the intel you need."

"Hold on!" said Surge, jumping to his feet. "Are you two fucking mad? Look at you. Both of you are eligible for bus passes and you plan to take on a firm of London villains? You are both geriatrics! What are you going to do Collins? Hit them with your zimmer frame?" He glared at both of them. "Twenty years ago we may have pulled this off, but get real!"

Collins looked at Surge, his face full of disappointment. After a pause he said, "I have to do this thing but I understand it is not your business." He stood up. "Thanks for coming," and he reached out to shake his hand. "Jon will run you home."

Surge looked away and walked towards the wall. He turned and looked at the two men, all colour gone from his face. "Will you still go on even without me?" he asked.

"Don't worry. It is none of your concern," replied Collins.

"Don't fucking tell me what is or is not my concern," shouted Surge. His face was now flushed and he was angry, spitting out the words. "You are out of your minds."

"I have to do it," said Collins. "It is my honour and my duty. I loved her and walked through most of my life with her. I cannot turn the other cheek."

Collins put his arm around Surge's shoulder and looked him straight in the eye. "Look," he said, softly. "If you want me to I can release you from your promise. You do not have to do this. I am sorry. I should not have asked you."

Surge's eyes filled with tears. His shoulders slumped. "Why did you ask me?" he asked.

"Because I have no one else and I need you," said Collins. "You were, you are, the best."

"Not anymore," said Surge in a flat voice.

"But still good enough," said The Grey Man.

Surge stared back and then sat down with a look of resignation on his face. He stared at the floor and after a few seconds said, "Fuck it, what else have I got to do?" Then he looked first at Collins then at The Grey Man, "Don't expect too much. Now what do you need?"

Collins smiled and then started to talk fast. "I want The Grey Man to track down the soldiers on the ground floor, the ones picking up the drugs. They will be the most sloppy and insecure and from them build up a picture of the organisation's hierarchy, work out patterns and routines and where to strike to disrupt and confuse. I am not interested in these foot soldiers just the ones pulling the strings."

"I want you Surge, once we have this intel, to hurt the body of the organisation, attack them, steal their drugs and set one against the other to drive the leaders out in the open. If possible get them to think another organisation is muscling in. Try to make them panic. Then we step in and destroy everything."

"In essence," said Collins pausing. "The plan is simple. Surge to disrupt, The Grey Man to plan and me to do the killing."

Jon looked at his father at that point and heard the chilling words. Gone was his dad. Gone was the shopkeeper. Gone was the man he knew. There stood a cold and ruthless killer. It frightened him to his core.

"Timescales?" asked The Grey Man.

"They must be watching me," said Collins, "After the murder they want to see what I will do, how I will react. Will I go to the police? Fight or roll over? It is essential for success and for Jon's sake, assuming he wants to lead a normal life in the future, that they have no understanding of what we are doing. I do not want any comeback after we are finished. Go in, wipe them out and disappear without anyone being the wiser."

"I would guess," he went on. "They will not give me too much time before they move in. I would suggest they will leave me for a month to stew, then contact me and ask for weekly payments which will increase steadily as they put the squeeze on, possibly for another couple of months, before I would have to agree to bring in the drugs. I want to move before that point. Altogether I think we have around three months to let the dust settle before we can strike."

"That works for me," said The Grey Man. "I can have the basic organisation outlined within eight weeks if nothing goes wrong. Then we have a month after that to plan."

Both men looked at Surge. "I know. I know," said Surge. "Three months to get fit. I can do it but will need a safe place to live and some back identity if people come checking."

"No problem," said Collins, smiling. "The flat is already let. Jon will take you there tonight."

They spent the next hour going through contact procedures and fallback positions. Collins handed Surge the flat address and a stiff, yellow envelope which he had prepared earlier. It contained £10,000 in cash for expenses. Everything would be cash for Surge from now on. No credit card tracking. Along with this was a driving licence, passport under the name Mark Emblem and a list of names he could give as references if he needed to.

The Grey Man reached into a battered old briefcase which had gone by almost unnoticed and handed out three smart phones and went through their functions and various speed dial numbers.

"How did you know to bring these?" asked Collins.

"Not difficult," replied The Grey Man. "Any op needs good communication." Surge guessed everything had come from The Firm as usual. Was there nothing you could not get from them he wondered?

Jon looked at them planning. Three old men. Each one older than the last - the drunk, the shop keeper and the geriatric. They looked so ordinary. Surge was just a bit bigger than most men but nothing special. All three were well past their sell by date, and it was unbelievable that they were going to take on an organised crime gang! It appeared an unfunny joke. The only suspicion that they could be capable of something more was when they were together. There was a sense of competence, of experience. A surety about their actions, somehow professional. Three skilled men going to work. Jon studied them closely. If he looked hard he could almost see the men they had been and it gave him a spark of hope but it passed quickly and he wondered what he was getting into, prison maybe or death. Whatever happens he knew he would not be the same person he was before his mother's murder but the youth in him rose to the adventure and he felt a burst of adrenalin course through his veins. He was going to war without any basic training. 'Fuck it!' he thought echoing Surge's words, 'Why not?'

Finally the old men stood and so did Jon. "From this moment on we are operational and all that means," said Collins. "Look to your back at all times." He poured four whiskies from a decanter and gave the toast,

"Who's like us? There's none like us. So here's to us!" The words sent a shiver down Jon's back.

Later Jon drove Surge to a small block of rundown flats in South London. Surge insisted they drove past and did a circuit around the block before stopping the car half a mile away. He stepped out the door and gave two raps on the roof before walking swiftly away without looking back.

Jon drove back through the dark, wet streets, his mind full of today. He got home and let himself in quietly so as not to wake his father. As he walked down the hall he saw him sitting in the lounge where he had met all those well wishers earlier.

"What did you think of my two friends?" he asked.

"Well," said Jon. "The Grey Man looked like a ghost."

"Which is what he is," said Collins. "The best intelligence gatherer I have ever worked with."

"OK," Jon said. "And you are some kind of assassin I suppose. So what does Surge do? Is he a communications guy or computer expert or something else?"

His father laughed, the only laugh of the long day. "No. He is a breaker."

"What's that?" asked Jon. "He breaks men," replied his father.

"Oh, like a fighter?" said Jon.

"No. Surge doesn't fight. He breaks," said Collins. "He takes men apart and breaks their bodies."

"Well, he looks to me like all he could break is the lid off a bottle!" said Jon laughing.

"Trust me," said his dad. "I have never known his like and he may surprise you yet."

Surge woke the next morning in a strange bed in a strange flat full of mixed emotions, some good, some bad and he sat at the table trying to understand them. The good he supposed was the fact that he did not have a hangover. Last night was the first night for five years, in fact since he had left hospital, that he had gone to bed without a drink. As well he realised he now had a sense of purpose, something to get up for and work for a feeling he had not had in a long while but this left him with the bad, and he realised it was guilt that Collins' wife had died to give him this mission to bring him back to life. He smiled, despite the guilt he was operational something he felt he would never feel again and relished the idea of pitting himself against other men as he had done all his life. The balance however in his mind was did he still have it or would he be the one broken again? He could still feel the pain of the cracked bones as the baseball bats smashed into his body. Time would tell.

He had met Collin's wife only once many, many years ago. She had been small and round and plain and nice, just ordinary. She obviously doted on Collins and their new son. In the world he lived in with Collins, The Grey Man and other strange people, the ordinariness of her had struck him. She understood but did not want to be any part of their mysterious world.

The need and determination that she had to bring up their child outside of the life that Collins was involved in, had made her very special, and unbelievably she had achieved it standing on her own, building up a her little business and keeping the filth of the spooks world from her and her son's door. A remarkable achievement.

She did not deserve to die like this and Surge would give Collins the room he needed to avenge her. Was she worth fighting and dying for, though, he asked himself. Was she worth his life? There was only one answer. Of course she was. She epitomised decency, honesty and the right to live your life your way. This was always worth fighting and if necessary dying for. Wickedness and evil should be opposed wherever you find them. He had made this choice all those years ago, set himself a code to live by, way before he had met the little man in borstal.

Chapter 3

The estate agent opened the door and stepped back to let the man go into the apartment first, and took the opportunity to discreetly scrutinise him. Tall, slim, good looking, 30 something, dressed in an immaculate handmade, Italian blue suit. He always sized up his customers to pigeon hole them into the have and have-nots. Those with new or old money. It was a game he liked to play, essential if you were to spot a trickster or con artist who were rife in London. He had a lifetime of experience behind him, working at the most expensive hotels, clubs and now as an exclusive estate agent always mixing at the top level in London's property market. It was a game started by his father who had been a butler to the aristocracy and had given him many tips on spotting a fake against the real thing.

'Never worry about the quality of the suit son,' he had explained. 'Any mug can spend a lot of money on that. It is the accessories you need to notice, the small details - the wrong cufflinks, shoes, socks, tie, etc, these will differentiate. Money always sets itself a level, a standard if you will, so if the suit is handmade, 99-100 times the shirt and shoes should be as well. Look for anomalies, the cheap tie with the Rolex watch, last year's shoes etc. It takes breeding and years of watching to fully understand, but if all is correct then you will be able to spot your man.'

New money of course was obvious but old money only stood out if you knew what to look for and Mr Lee looked old money. So he studied him as carefully but discreetly as he could. The shirt was cream, Egyptian cotton, definitely handmade but not Jermyn Street, unusual as that was the preferred option. It took him a few seconds to realise that the shade was almost too perfect a match for the suit, not a standard cream colour, so the suit tailor had made the shirt to match perfectly, a lovely touch, showing detail. Class as well as money. The shoes definitely Lobbs of London, at least £2000; cufflinks plain old gold and well used, that fits, and a beautiful stylish 1930's French watch just peeping out from the cuff as he bent his arm. Stunning. The collar of the shirt was undone, no tie which was becoming very fashionable in the City and the hair was slightly too long, parted in the middle with two bangs either side of the face which made him look younger and stopped the whole outfit from looking 'too much'. Everything was very expensively styled and he had obviously spent time abroad as the tan complemented the shirt exactly. It took him almost no time to come to his decision. 'Yes, Mr Lee you are pukka,' he thought. 'Definitely the genuine article.'

Lee smiled to himself knowing the game and the fact he had 'passed muster'. 'Why not?' he thought. 'I am the real thing'. Born into an old aristocratic family which could trace its lineage back to William the Conqueror, he had been brought up in a huge house with sprawling landscapes. But like so many others today, he had the bad fortune to be born to a family who were asset rich but cash poor. His father had tried all his life to change their circumstances and finally after many years of hard work, investing in various different schemes, he achieved a result. Unfortunately they were now asset poor as well as cash poor, losing almost everything but the name, just as Lee had graduated from school and gone to Sandhurst Military Academy.

His upbringing had been a farce pretending to be wealthy whilst living on hand-me-downs and credit, his family ridiculed by those in the know. At Sandhurst it was worse. Lee became a follower, living off his peers, never able to reciprocate the meals and drinks and parties, pretending not to hear the snide remarks and laughing along with the others at his fate. He had hated it and vowed to get money from somewhere.

And here he was in Kensington at a very upmarket address, looking round the large set of apartments with the thick beige carpets and expensive, albeit fake Georgian furniture, everything beautifully styled and immaculate. The right apartment with the right look in the right place, not original but smelling of money just as he liked it. Here was a place to impress, to pay back all the ridicule of his youth, the poor rich boy done good.

He wandered over to the window and looked out over London, a beautiful view. Below in the private spot was parked his immaculate 1966 Porsche 911 looking perfectly in place. Without turning and looking at the estate agent he asked, "How much?"

The Estate Agent smiled and licked his lips. "For a six month lease, it is £60,000 with a further £20,000 as a deposit." There was a pause almost for the drama of the sum. "Fine," said Lee. "I'll transfer the money in the morning and move in on Saturday."

"Perfect," said the Estate Agent and took out the paperwork to be signed. "I hope you will enjoy your stay," he continued, almost meaning it.

Lee walked out the large door and down the wide steps to the dark green Porsche, the only colour to have for that year. It had been completely restored and looked brand new. He opened the door and climbed into the beautiful leather interior. The car wrapped around him like a blanket. Once inside, his mind went back to how he had got here from pauper to almost rich.

After passing out from Sandhurst, the army had sent him as a young officer to Pakistan and Afghanistan patrolling the borders which even today were still quite wild and lawless, specialising in the drug trafficking and terrorism industries that had been prevalent here before Christ was born. Lee's job was mundane, working on policing borders and guarding supply chains to the field troops. Every now and then, a sortie in an armoured convoy to show the natives what's what.

Boredom overcame him quickly and more as a way of passing the time he started to learn the local languages, picking each one up easily. From the language came the culture and the contacts. His senior officers soon realised what an asset this was and used him more and more for liaison between the various gangs and war chiefs, all of whom turned out to be valuable contacts for Lee. They soon learned that Lee liked cash and the good life and was always interested in earning more. They were an inventive people, used to bribing officials so they started to ask for certain favours such as turning a blind eye as certain convoys came through or advance notice of raids on drug routes. All very lucrative for Lee.

He was then introduced to Mick Smith, an amoral supply sergeant who was selling guns and ammo direct from stores to the locals. They got on like a house on fire. Smith, from the back streets of London and Lee from the aristocracy set and Sandhurst - between them they covered all of society. Lee had him transferred to his platoon and they started to build their empire piece by piece. Smith had no qualms about what he did to make money or gain influence. He was a born sadist, an excellent marksman and he would often take commissions to kill rival troublemakers or chieftains using his snipers rifle, with Lee there to get him out of trouble if things went south. In a short space of time the two of them started to own the region, organising and controlling, making just enough trouble and arrests to keep them posted whilst a smooth drug trade developed within agreed set limits not large enough to set off alarms.

Everything in the region quietened down and the politicians were delighted. In fact both the army and the local drug dealers thought it was an ideal situation. Things were going well but it was not the 'big time;. The money they were earning was good just not enough for Lee's ambitions. He needed a big score and when it came it proved to be easier than he thought.

He had heard enough complaints from the drug barons to know that the main drug problem was not the growing or refining of the heroin, it was the getting it safely to the West in large enough and pure enough quantities to make it worthwhile. Everything that could be tried, had been tried - using human mules, hiding it in various cars, containers, boats, etc, but the Customs men had become more and more sophisticated at finding it. Time and again a path had been opened then Customs had found out, the supply stopped and the network crashed until new methods could be employed.

Lee worried about the problem from all ends. He felt there must be a solution, if only he could just find it, until one day whilst visiting a small local produce shop he had an epiphany. He saw that the owner was parcelling up a small quantity of a local narcotic herb with a postage address in London. Lee asked the man how many parcels he sent to London.

"Only a couple per month to an old friend who sells it in his corner shop to his locals," he replied.

"Any issues with Customs?" asked Lee.

"No," said the man. "They are only after the big deals. I could send anything if I wanted to. Who would waste their time on a parcel this size? It is like a drop in the ocean."

So Lee, acting quite innocently as an English Officer who was interested in his area, took time to visit his local Customs office. The man in charge, flattered to be the centre of the English Officer's attention, was pleased to show him around and talked at great length about his department and all the processes in place. He moaned that It was clear to everyone they were under-resourced and had no time to inspect everything. There were hundreds of parcels and two Customs officers to police the lot.

"How do you cope with so much work with so few staff?" Lee asked.

"We can't," he said. "All we do is look for patterns, same parcel, same place, same day and we also look for differences, anything out of place or new or different, that's where we concentrate our resources."

"What about the small businessman who sends herbs abroad?" asked Lee.

"We check them out at the beginning," he replied. "Then maybe once or twice a year after that if we can. They are no trouble and at best what could we find? Next to nothing. Not worth the time and trouble."

From there it was easy. Lee had found his way.

Chapter 4

Surge sat in the dingy flat. It had a tiny kitchen with pealing browny cream lino, a small front room with windows down one side, bathroom and bedroom painted in a dirty yellow with a brown shaggy carpet. He sat on the corner of the bed opposite a long mirror with the silver flaking off the back. Everything was old and faded. 'Like me' he thought. He stared at his face. An old man looked back at him, salt and pepper hair, thinning on top, fat face with small eyes, bloodshot cheeks and a red drinker's nose down to a double chin. He looked every day of his age. On impulse he stood up and took off his shirt. Below was a pasty body, fat arms, man boobs and a beer gut. 'How had he let himself get into this state?' he wondered. His mind went back over the years to when the World was young.

He was born into a petty criminal's family in East London and lived his early life in a rundown council house on one of the large lawless estates. His dad was known as one of the" chaps" working with, but on the periphery of, the major gangs of that time, always ducking and diving, trying to make a dishonest living in the 1950s and 60s, constantly in and out of jail. He thought himself a" hard man" and was quick to jump on anything that reinforced that impression. Most nights he held court at the local pub telling stories of his exploits, and lived on his reputation but was very careful not to cross the big boys. He knew his place and when to show it. When Surge was around five or six years old a group of families had come together in the back garden of one of the gang leader's houses. It was supposed to be a family barbecue but quickly became a place of hard drinking and gambling, betting on anything they could think of, everyone was bragging about this and that. Then someone had an idea on what would be great to bet on. Surge was sent for. He was to fight another boy, a son of another gang member and the money was laid down. The odds were on the bigger older boy 5-1 and Surge's dad, a gut full of beer and bluster, threw down £50, almost a week's wages that he could ill afford. "That's for my son," he said.

The other boy was about two years older and full of confidence and it started off as a quick wrestle and tussle fight but soon got nastier. Something in Surge came alive that day and his temper flew. A red rage came down and he quickly became vicious and even though the other boy was stronger and larger Surge had the will and the heart. At the end he found himself on top of the boy who was by now laying flat on his back on the ground. Surge was punching his face over and over as the boy cried, begging him to stop. Surge was finally dragged off and his dad was ecstatic. He carried him round the garden on his shoulders, victorious waving his winnings in his right hand.

Two days after his dad took him to a small gym and he was given boxing lessons by a kindly old pro and part time bouncer. Surge loved it for the discipline, the fear he felt in the ring fighting bigger boys and for the exercise which pushed his young body to the limit. He took to it like duck to water. By the time he was eight years old Surge was entered into all kinds of amateur boxing tournaments, never losing. He was a phenomenon and many people had high hopes for him but just as he reached ten years old his father was caught again by the police and was given five years for robbing a jewellery shop. Surge found himself alone with his mother, a fey woman who only cared for herself. He shopped, cooked and sorted the house out while she sat watching TV or out with her cronies. No money was coming into the house except from the dole and boxing had to go. The old man was kind but fees had to be paid.

Surge grew up real quick then, quite surprisingly to some. Bearing in mind his background and poverty, his school work was exemplary. He was bright and hard working. He tried as hard at school as he did out of it and did well. The only downside was that for some reason Surge struggled to make any friends. There was a touch of violence about him even at that age and other boys avoided him. He was a lonely solitary child, growing old before his time.

Most evenings he would walk home, cook tea and do his homework and then wander the streets to keep away from his mother. On one of these nights he passed a small church hall and heard inside the grunts and screams of a karate club. The door was open to let the cool air in. He crept in with it and sat at one of the benches, just off the dojo floor. He was enthralled with the moves, the mats, the discipline and even the smell. That first night Surge sat completely still for the two hours the lesson lasted watching as the pupils worked with the instructors.

After the discipline of boxing where only hands are used the freedom of fighting with your whole body struck a chord in his mind and after leaving as quietly as he came, danced home throwing kicks and punches into the night. For the next two weeks he went back there every night watching the different ages of pupils come and go, from the early evening children class through to 7.00pm when the adults arrived training late into the evening. He studied the steps, watched the moves and was completely absorbed.

One night the owner and chief instructor came over and sat next to him.

"What do you think?" he asked.

"Fantastic," said Surge.

"Then why not join in?" said the instructor.

"I have no money for lessons or a karate suit," replied Surge and quietly explained his situation as the instructor listened, looking at this earnest young boy with shabby clothes and scuffed shoes.

"Where do you live?" said the instructor and Surge gave his address. "Let me see what I can do," and he moved back onto the dojo floor.

The next night as Surge got home from school he found the instructor sitting in the kitchen talking to his mother. She said, "Do you want to do this martial art thing?"

Surge just nodded and the instructor said, "I have agreed with your mother that you will help me around the dojo cleaning and fixing things in exchange for lessons as long as your school work is kept up." Surge knew this had come from the instructor as his mother didn't care what he did but he just smiled and said, "Sure. Great. Anything you need."

That evening he turned up at the hall and the instructor gave him a new gi martial art suit and explained he was to call him Sensei which means teacher. He then put Surge through a few warm up exercises. As the class started Surge was placed at the back copying the other children as they moved up and down the dojo throwing kicks and punches. After ten minutes the instructor sent a brown belt down to work with Surge showing him some of the stances and how to move. Like the boxing, it came ridiculously easy to him. Surge relished the detail, the repetition of the strikes, kicks and blows, trying for perfection in each move. He liked controlling his body making it do what he wanted. For the next few years it became the centre of his life. Every waking moment was about training and the martial arts pushing his mind and body, watching everything he ate and drunk, following rigorous stretching and body building techniques. He would stay after each class had finish, endlessly going over a routine or sometimes just a small move searching for that perfection, delighting when he got it right. In the dojo he had found his home and his purpose. He hardly spoke to anyone around him just pushed himself way beyond what a boy of that age should be doing, looking for new techniques, honing his balance, suppleness and strength.

As he grew older he moved into the adult class two or three years before he should have and sensei's from other clubs would travel to train and spar with him, pushing him ever further. Life was school, homework then dojo then school, homework, dojo. Weekends were training and working on the chores at the club. In his Sensei he had found a second father and a family in the club, complete with moral codes and rules - honesty, decency, strength, patience and understanding. He not only learned to fight but how to control himself, how to think and how to live his life.

At 14 he looked 18 tall and powerful with a mature steady outlook. If he lacked anything it was maybe a sense of humour and the ability to mix easily with others. He had become a very serious young man.

Then his mother died - not of any major disease. She just seemed to give up and Surge found her one evening in the kitchen slumped over the table, a little middle- aged woman who just looked worn out. At the time he felt little. It was only later in life when he was older and a little wiser he found room for sorrow and what might have been.

The powers-that -be in the social services thought Surge was too young to live on his own so the prison service let his father out early. The life Surge now had, suited his dad. Surge was hardly home and when he was he took care of himself, washing, cooking and cleaning. He just needed a few pounds a week and that was fine, no responsibility at all, so his dad immediately went back to his old ways, some thieving and a few jobs for the boys meant money was easy come, easy go.

Then one night about three months after his mum's death and his father's release, Surge came home and was cornered by his dad smelling strongly of beer.

"I need your help," he said.

"Doing what?" said Surge.

"You just need to keep a watch out for me. I am going to turnover that jewellery shop that got me into prison last time. The owner got me five years. He needs to pay."

Surge said he wouldn't do it but his dad insisted.

"If you don't you can piss off!" he shouted. "No more money, no house, nothing!"

Surge shrugged, looked his dad in the eyes and went to pack. His dad then came into the bedroom and sat Surge down.

"Look son," he said. "I have never asked you for anything, just this one job and just as a lookout. I need you," he wheedled. "Please son I need someone I can trust to watch my back. I am in big trouble with some bad men and without this money I could get seriously hurt."

Surge finally agreed. He had no choice. He could not bear to see his old man hurt but he insisted only as a lookout.

"Just one job, just one job," his father kept saying.

Needless to say it was a complete mess, a set up. His dad had been drinking the night before and told a mate in confidence, who then told someone, who told someone else who told the police. Both of them were caught - his dad going in for another five year stretch. Surge was taken into care and then pushed around from one remand centre to the next. His Sensei and other members of the club stepped in as character references but Surge had nowhere to go so was finally sent to borstal.

Surge thought of that first night in borstal as he lay on the bed in the scruffy safe house. It had been a defining moment in his life. Borstal was a prison for children and just as frightening as any adult institution, with locks and bars and uniforms. As he walked in he could see the eyes of the other boys on him, thirteen year olds up to seventeen, tough grim looking faces, not one smile. Surge knew this was a hard place. His dad had told him about prison. "There is a pecking order" he said. "You have to stand up and be counted or be someone else's property. Better to take a beating than be a pussy."

Surprisingly when Surge looked inside himself that night he did not feel fear just anticipation. He had been fighting as long as he could remember but only for sport. He had always wondered if the techniques he had learnt would really work outside the dojo. Tonight he would find out, whatever happened blood would flow. He felt his heartbeat rise and his body flush with adrenaline.

After his talk with the senior security officer who read him the rules, he collected blankets, towels and soap. They went into the institution's sleeping dormitory, white walls and black and white lino everywhere with bars on the windows. It smelt of cabbage and greens and bleach. He saw the rows of iron framed beds, some empty, some with boys on reading or watching him. He deliberately chose one in the corner between two double deck framed bunk beds, and he saw some of the bigger, tougher looking boys smile. No way out, they thought he was trapped.

He lay on the top bunk and pretended to sleep but when the lights went out he moved down between the beds with his back to the wall, the bunk beds both side protecting his flanks. Any boy trying to get to him would have to climb over the lower bunk leaving them awkward, crouched and un-protected. How many he wondered two - three - four - anticipation grew. Then he saw them in the gloom stealing towards him, six of the biggest and oldest. He also could feel the rest of the dorm awake waiting to pile in when he went down.

The big leader pushed to the front, almost a man at 6ft and 14 stone. As he moved round into the gap between the beds, in the gloom he quietly said "You are mine you little shit." Surge smiled and sent a front kick that snapped under his jaw knocking him out. He collapsed and the boy behind tripped over the body. Surge sent two quick hard punches smashing into his face, blood from his nose sprayed out. Then Surge attacked. The last thing any of them thought he would do. All the boys were street fighters but Surge was that and much, much more. His body was hard and powerful, trained how to strike and where, his technique honed from years of repetition and practice. In those moments he was like a berserker and even these tough vicious boys stepped back from his fury. He left all six cowering and weeping having ensured each one had at least one bone broken. The bigger lad who had attacked first got it worse suffering a rib, arm and broken leg. Surge had sent out a strong loud message.

Then he sent out another. He walked down the dormitory looking each boy in the eye, blood on his face, T-shirt and trousers and blood dripping from both hands - none of it his. "Anyone else want to have a go?" he said. "ANYONE?" As he spoke he turned around full circle. No one replied, no one moved, no one caught his eye. They all knew an alpha male when they saw one. Surge's temper, his ability and his willingness to fight holding nothing back, frightened them all, a tiger amongst jackals.

The borstal staff heard the commotion and charged in. They saw the bodies and the mess and walked up to Surge who by now was sitting on his bed. "What happened?" they asked. "No idea," replied Surge.

No one talked to the authorities as was the way but they could guess and after a dressing down from the governor, Surge was allowed back into the main stream. The governor realised that it would have looked ridiculous to suggest that one fourteen year old year old beat off six almost men. He decided Surge probably had done him a favour. He put the incident down officially to a gang fight and transferred all the broken boys to another borstal.

Surge was a known man after that and was left alone. He eventually teamed up with some other lads, the better types, and they worked together watching each other's backs. Surge had only two other fights in the next two years from new arrivals, older bigger lads who did not believe his reputation. He beat them both, then systematically broke their arms.

Both these incidents were also overlooked as Surge caused no trouble and even helped in lessons. By law the borstal had to educate the kids but normally the classes were noisy and no one paid attention to the teacher who was just going through the motions. Surge stopped that. He wanted and needed to learn. Every class that Surge attended was quiet and orderly so much so that the borstal started to improve their school marks much to the governor's pleasure. Surge settled into a life of routine, building his mind and his body.

Chapter 5

Lee met with Smith two days after the meeting with the Customs Officer and started to work out the details. They needed to get the drug barons to provide the drugs and to prepare the parcels, something he was sure they would be happy to do. Then they had to infiltrate the small legitimate businesses in Pakistan and Afghanistan who were already sending parcels to the UK using either bribery or coercion, or a bit of both, and convince them to cooperate in also sending their product, as well as ensuring the receivers would play ball. Lee suggested they start there. Then when they got back to London they could start collecting the goods build the stock and begin to investigate the plethora of other ethnic businesses to send the small parcels to, so allowing the expansion he needed into the big time.

The local, small businessmen were relatively easy to persuade, one way or another many had family in the UK who would also agree to receive and hold the parcels until Lee and Smith got back and collected them. Most were compliant, already paid some kind of protection money and knew better than to go to the police. In fact to them, Lee was the police. Once the deal was done, Lee assured them that no one would be asked to send too much or too frequently, little and far between per shopkeeper was best. Work the odds at all times. No patterns, no large shipments. Lee was sure Smith could deal with any overzealous Custom officers either with money or broken bones.

London was the difficult bit - he needed to find someone who wanted what he had now to sell. Smith had the answer he always been on the edge of the law - the army was supposed to make an honest man of him. He grew up in a shady part of London and knew from the old days a money man called Stevens who had his finger in every pie and knew everyone in the underworld worth knowing . He called in a favour from an old friend and arranged a meeting so Lee flew to London on his next leave.

The meeting was set in the City of London, in a large impressive building which smelt of money and privilege. It took a while to get to see Stevens. Lee sat in the waiting room for hours, way beyond the meeting time set. It was obviously a lesson in humility, but once Lee managed to get into the office, Stevens was all ears. Lee's pitch was simple and to the point.

"I have as much heroin as this city can handle and a way of getting it here uncut. All I need to expand is collection and distribution."

"What do you need from me?" asked Stevens.

"Money," said Lee. "A way of laundering many millions of pounds and contacts into distribution. Can you help?"

Stevens smiled a big cheesy smile, "What do you offer?" he asked.

"A three way split on all profits with me and Smith," said Lee.

Stevens, a large, greedy man jumped at the opportunity and readily agreed. "As long as there was a firewall between him, the drugs and the operation," he said. "Just money in and money out as usual." As he liked to say 'he could launder more money than the bank of England.' They shook hands. The deal was done.

"Now let's discuss my contacts in distribution" Stevens said.

London was not managed by one big crime group. Each area had its own organisation and hierarchy, buying drugs where they could and distributing them throughout the clubs, pubs and drinking dens. Infighting between organisations was discouraged as a low profile was called for and wars were expensive.

Stevens explained that because of what he offered in the way of money laundering he knew all the top boys and also knew that the timing of Lee's proposal could not come at a better time as there was currently a problem with the drug trade which Lee's deal would be able to solve.

"Dilution dear boy that is the issue it is ruining the business, cutting as everyone knows is the secret to making money," he said. "Buy in a quantity, add some talcum powder or bleach or anything else to hand

and you have your profit. However because of today's, convoluted route to get to London, the drugs coming here currently will have passed through too many hands, all cutting it to make their bit. Sometimes if they are not careful by the time it hit the streets there is hardly any heroin left, not good for business. Pure heroin though directly in London would be a dream come true and worth a fortune to anyone who could get their hands on it."

Stevens set up a meeting the following Monday afternoon in his London office for the four main gangs. They arrived early, but Stevens as was his way wanted to let them stew. Lee paced up and down the expensive white carpet as he waited.

"Relax," said Stevens. "This will be easy."

"Are these the four leaders?" asked Lee.

"No" said Stevens. "They would never meet for fear of a trap. But these are trusted members, just pitch them as you did me."

When Stevens was ready, they both walked into the plush meeting room. A large thick mahogany desk with flowers and a tray with a decanter of water and glasses were in the centre. The walls were covered in old masters. Everything looked expensive and refined. Lee however was a touch disappointed. He expected villains from TV, dealer boots and thick sheepskin coats, the archetypal crook. Instead he got four businessmen, all with dark suits and open collared shirts, two had laptops open, all were chatting freely like old friends. It could have been a business meeting anywhere. Lee started by placing a small parcel on the table. It was silver in colour and sealed with tape, the sort you might get at an expensive chocolate shop with half a dozen chocolates inside.

"Gentlemen," Lee began. "I would like to sell you all the drugs you can handle, uncut." They all smiled.

"How?" one of them asked.

"By filling these up at source and sending them to my contacts all over London," he said holding up the parcel.

"Are you kidding?" said a medium sized, well spoken man closest to the door. "What can that hold? A few grams?"

"a bit more," said Lee. "But what if I sent hundreds of these parcels every week?"

"You would get caught by Customs," said the same man. "They look for such shipments."

"Sure, if they go to the same place," said Lee. "But what if they went to 100 different addresses and then next week a 100 different ones and so on? No pattern."

"It would mean that the product would have to support too many people being paid for too little merchandize, not cost effective, and an organisation so big that someone would talk," the man replied.

"Agreed," said Lee smiling. "But what if the people who received such parcels were not part of an organisation but were individuals, say foreigners with connections back to their home country who may, quite legitimately, receive lots of parcels from home and every now and then one of ours?"

Suddenly the penny dropped and they all lent forward.

Lee continued leaning forward his face now serious . "Have you any idea how many Indian, Asian, Pakistani, Afghanis, live and work in London? There are millions! Most of them will have ties to home. They don't want police interference in their lives. Some will take the parcels willingly for a small sum, a few will need to be lent on. Remember the risk to them is small. Even if they got caught, it would be an isolated incident and they can swear the parcel was not theirs, just a big mistake."

"I have set up the source end and am currently putting together the London network of receivers. I will start to expand this London end very quickly, within a few months shipping significant volume which will grow as we move forward. All I need from you is pick up, processing and distribution. I do not need to tell you this small box increases in value substantially with some clever cutting."

"How much?" said a thin man opposite to Lee.

Lee said a price close to what they were paying today for cut heroin. It meant the profits for each member would increase ten-fold. Lee knew a terrific deal for everyone in that room as why buy cut when you can buy uncut for the same price?

Suddenly, there were smiles all round. It was a eureka moment for all sitting there chairs were pushed back and excitement filled the air. The rest of the time went by with question after question. Logistics, communication, dividing up the areas etc, all very civilised and controlled with points conceded and gained just like any other business meeting. They could have been talking about almost any product. Lee thought it quite bizarre.

The only awkward part came when they were discussing the current drug suppliers who would be frozen out as Lee upped quantities and his organisation expanded.

"I will need protection," Lee argued. "This is too big for it to be screwed up by a rival group."

The four associates all smiled and assured him that these people would be taken care of and nothing would come back to him. He decided not to ask for details of how that would happen.

After a couple of hours everything looked to be in order and all four looked at each other, then at Lee. "We have a deal," they said, and rose to shake his hand.

Now Lee could collect what had already been sent and open the channel, sending package after package to his friendly contacts in London. He then started to expand the receiving network by approaching any small businesses in Pakistan and on the border who also had family in London. On some he would offer a straight payment deal, on others he would threaten friends and family, and on any who resisted he would just used strong arm tactics. Smith joined in with the strong stuff. He liked that.

Lee spent much of his time back and forwards to London, Pakistan and Afghanistan, building and strengthening his network. He had resigned his commission and started working out how to expand.

Smith's time was nearly up in the Army and he joined him three months later quickly becoming the muscle man. It was not long before they had perfected the system with the London gangs keeping the pressure on the receivers, picking up the packages, cutting and distributing with all money for the drugs paid in advance to Stevens.

As promised, the existing suppliers were taken out by the various gangs. Some went quietly, plying their trade elsewhere. Some disappeared completely. Lee was going to be the only game in town.

Twelve months later they had two hundred and twenty seven small businessmen supplying a few grams to half a kilo each per month into the pot across London, which quickly added up to millions of pounds. Lee was generous ensuring the drug manufactures got the cash quickly and on time and the London gangs were often over supplied. Everybody got rich. Three years later it showed significant growth and the system was working so well drugs were even being exported into Europe through what Customs would see as the back door. They were looking for drugs coming into London, not going out.

A few shopkeepers had been caught but all they pleaded a lack of knowledge of the parcel and, with no criminal or drugs track record, all they received was a slap on the wrist and some preliminary investigation from the police. During this time Lee would rest them for a few months until Customs and the police got bored watching them. Then they started all over again.

In those past three years there had not been one major hiccup, not one major problem and they now owned most of London.

The only issue to the real 'big time' was getting more and more receivers. He was working on that today with a big meeting planned, but Smith was worrying him, he was pushing too hard and Lee wondered about the woman shopkeeper he had shot. Smith had argued that she was going to the police and he had to do it but she had a son and Lee was sure some pressure there would have kept her quiet. Shootings in London are relatively rare and can attract a lot of attention from the police which they did not need. He had a bad feeling about it all but he put it to the back of his mind and smiled to himself. If today went well, he was finally going to make it.

Lee had been extremely careful about keeping both sides - manufacturing and distribution – separate. They both needed him and wanted him to be kept alive and supplying. For Lee it was perfect, the whole operation outsourced, with Stevens laundering the money off shore.

He estimated he had about two years before it got so big it would either be found out by the police or one of his partners would get greedy and cut him out. He needed to time it carefully, when to sell out and jump himself. But he had one more big deal before he sold out.

Chapter 6

After Surge and Jon had left the meeting, The Grey Man stayed on for another hour talking through with Collins everything he had found out so far about the organisation and what he planned to do next. There was no envelope for him, he had more than enough money. Finally after checking out of the window all was clear, he slipped down the back stairs of the apartment, took a quick look left and right, then walked three quarters of a mile changing direction often and sometimes back tracking as was his want. He did this more by reflex and habit than any great worry he was being followed but as he had hunted and been hunted all his life, constantly operational, these habits kept him alive.

Once satisfied he was clear, he approached a grey Ford Mondeo owned by The Firm. The Grey Man had never used it before. He took out his phone dialling six digits and holding it to his ear. This was a special number for that car and it activated a radio signal that opened the door lock remotely. At the same time as dialling, he reached into his pocket and pulled out some keys pretending to activate a car fob for anyone watching. The central locking popped the door opened. He got into the driving seat and reached across into the glove compartment where he took out the real car keys, swiftly inserted them into the ignition and drove away.

The Grey man loved The Firm. Even the name 'The Firm' was a misnomer. There was not one company but a myriad of companies all loosely joined together. It had provided the bulk of The Grey Man's work for the past thirty years and the reason for his vast wealth.

In the late 1960s with the cold war at its height, The UK intelligence service was a huge industry, employing tens of thousands of people. Very few were in the front line, the bulk being the quiet individuals who lived, on the face of it, ordinary lives both in the UK and abroad and, when called for, could supply certain services - cars in

Berlin, safe houses in Manchester, documents of all types - whatever was needed to support the front line operative.

However, the costs were incredible. For example, paying someone to live in France and adopt a low profile existence, who was possibly only called on for services twice a year was unbelievably expensive and inefficient. By the early 1970s the financial strain on the UK department was destroying it. With the three day working week and huge unemployment throughout the country, there was not the money to run an effective Secret Service and the department came close to closing down.

The Grey Man and others, including Collins, came up with a solution. Why not outsource all this infrastructure, set up the current security individuals in legitimate business, then when needed the security services would pay for the 'special service'. The rest of the time there would be no cost. It was a godsend. Small investments were made to a large number of staff along with, where possible, Government contracts to help them grow. This created a plethora of entrepreneurs who had a chance to earn some good legitimate money in whatever company they set up and charge exorbitantly for "special" services as needed. Most of these people had some operational experience and had been hired for their resourcefulness. They took to business like ducks to water with a nice, financial side line in security supply, all covered by the Official Secrets Act, each licensed by the government and some with European licences. As the UK joined the EU the whole scheme was run out through friendly EU governments.

The rules were simple - no deals with foreign governments who were not in the scheme, no dealings with terrorists or organised crime. Any lack of discretion would lead to expulsion, imprisonment or death.

The Grey Man had worked on the security aspects, constantly refining and improving them, keeping The Firm and everyone in it secret, creating distance and firewalls between suppliers and customers.

The latest incarnation involved the internet and everything now was processed on-line.

The Firm was set up for government use but such was the shady world it dealt with, there were also private special customers who were semi-official, essentially acting on their own and could be disowned. New laws forcing governments to be more open with the public, caused more so called 'private clients' to be set up.

To be a private client of The Firm, operating within the charter, but maybe to the left or right of various official Government policies, an individual needed to deposit a minimum of £1 million in a Swiss account. This allowed access to all services after extensive checks on their bona fides. Dropping below the £1 million meant expulsion, possibly never to return. Most of these specials, had tens of millions of pounds on deposit and conducted significant operations utilising the select services of The Firm.

Everything had a standard price called the rule of ten, normally ten times the retail cost of getting the product, if you could acquire it legally. For example, car hire that would cost legitimately £75 from Hertz or Avis a day, would cost £750 a day, drop off and pick up within 4 hours of a specified time unless other arrangements needed to be made at extra cost. These cars came with one off false, but legal number plates and road tax which would be disposed of after use and the car sold on with original plates and original road tax licence after a thorough steam clean and valet to security standards rendering forensics useless. If, however, there was a specific need, the car would be crushed and disposed of. The cost for this was of course ten times the retail value of the car.

Apartments were ten times the normal rent with security cleaning and for ten times more, full disposal of bodies, if necessary. Very lucrative for The Firm. Very convenient for the customer.

All documents were legitimate government sanctioned but on a strict time limit, utilising a back door system from security printers who would overrun specific base documents, the details filled in on-line, so paper and hard security devices were all legit and very useful. There was even a program that allowed a backdated register on official data bases if the document had to come from Government sources. If anyone checked, these documents were real. The back dates would expire after set dates to ensure no traceability.

The car opening device was one of The Grey Man's designs. He specialised in using everyday technology for covert use. In this case he had added alongside the infa-red switch on a normal central locking system, a radio control switch, which he set to a unique number. This number when dialled on a mobile phone opened the doors. Very simple but effective, meaning that you did not have to find keys or have them sent. You could use any Firm car with a minimum of fuss and time lost. At the end of the hire you put the keys into the glove box, got out ,phoned a different number which would lock the car and take the GPS record of where the call was made from. The Firm then dispatched someone to collect. All parking and speeding tickets were taken care of as part of the service. This system was now used on all Firm cars and he received a significant design fee.

To contact The Firm was simple. Initially through an encrypted web page with the encryption constantly changing, the customer had to use a special laptop or mobile phone which was synchronised with The Firm, most had fingerprint reading, and also a custom designed retina scan built into the camera.

The customer typed in their needs and the request was given a code number which was bounced round a number of hubs before arriving at the controller's desk who checked the security system to ensure everything was correct. However, he would not know the name or address of the customer, just the number and the fact they were kosher. The customer did not know the controller, ensuring absolute anonymity on both sides.

The controller read the request and then looked for companies in the area that could supply the specific needs. These were numbered again so he had no idea who he was dealing with, just that they offered the service required and were approved. He/she then contacted the company through an encrypted email server, set up the service that had been requested by the customer and then sent them whatever they needed, e.g. telephone numbers, addresses of safe houses, front and fall back places.

Now dealing directly with the controller but through many firewalls, the customer on a specific operation could ask for anything. Weapons to passports, cars to caravans, flight tickets to money and credit cards, membership of clubs and casinos, clean up teams and bodyguards, of course all at a price, all paid for in advance from the deposit.

It was an incredible system. Almost foolproof. There had been some problems in the early days but no more than when the system was run by the Government. The biggest issue facing The Firm today was that the original founders were getting old and finding replacements with the same skills was becoming hard. The Grey Man and Collins were very active in recruiting ,training and lecturing.

The Grey Man's biggest problem however was his success. He knew everything there was to know about the Firm including names of the players and so was a potential security risk. For the past ten years he had been hunted for this knowledge. But the rewards for him intellectually and financially had been immense.

Chapter 7

The Grey Man drove for two hours out into the countryside doubling back often and using side roads, then stopping and checking passing traffic. When he was satisfied he was alone, he stopped the car and activated the phone PDA, getting onto the internet and through a coded page, into the security system for the latest safe house he was using. He scanned through the CCTV system looking for anything suspicious. Everything looked fine, there had been no intruders nor was anything out of place. Next he looked at the system itself.

The cameras on the outside of his house were easily identifiable to anyone and were of a high standard but even a good system like this one could be bypassed by someone who knew what they were doing, sending the signals elsewhere and replacing them with dummy feeds. The Grey Man was aware of this and had deliberately designed the system to be challenging but not impossible. Once through the first firewall and into the system the hacker would think he was in charge. However, The Grey Man had a backup system looking for just this eventuality. It scanned the first for any interference, notifying The Grey Man and then switched on other covert surveillance systems. This backup was far more sophisticated than the overt one, it traced the hacker as well as bringing on other devices infa-red and motion detectors all built back into the walls and invisible. A system within a system. The overt system would be just challenging enough to fool anyone trying to break in and visible enough to show a high level of security. The covert stuff was the real safety net.

It was one of his signatures to hide one system inside another, to allow the perpetrator to think they had won, had cracked the puzzle and then not look any further.

After a ten minute scan showing everything was clear, The Grey Man drove on, activating the tall, steel ornate gate as he pulled into the driveway of what used to be a large, old farmhouse. He had converted it extensively over the past 18 months and calculated he had another 18 months before moving on again, which was as long as he ever felt safe in one place. Many men were hunting him and he was never more than a few steps ahead, always planning the next move. He had already bought a large house on The Rhine in Germany complete with cellar which was currently being converted by The Firm to his special requirements. It housed a secret exit with access to a fast boat.

The name he was known as here was Mr Graham. He doubted that his enemies would see him as a man with a sense of humour but thought that next time he must try something less able to be linked with his moniker.

He walked through the large, gothic style wooden front door to an immaculate hallway, beautifully decorated with a deep beige carpet, mahogany panelled walls, a large mahogany staircase with landscape oil pictures on the front wall. At the bottom of the stairs was an antique grandfather clock and a superb hanging tapestry on the side wall. From the front door the house looked expensive, old and lived in.

In fact it was a sham. Only the hall and front room were furnished. All the other rooms were bare except for dark curtains on the windows to stop anyone looking in. The hall and front room were for nosy neighbours, those who could not be ignored as complete isolation would have caused gossip. 'Blend in. Not stand out,' was his watchword. The Grey Man portrayed himself to these neighbours as a businessman who travelled and was home infrequently. He liked his privacy and dissuaded contact but was always polite and pleasant.

The only rooms The Grey Man used were in the basement behind a false wall. Here was housed his precious computers and his kitchen, bathroom and bed.

He switched on the main computer using the fingerprint and eye scan security system plus a password. The finger print and eye scan on their own would allow limited entry stopping most hackers from doing more. The system would look as if it was opening up and all files were accessible. But if the password was not instantly typed all that could be copied or downloaded was a nasty virus with The Grey Man's computer completely wiped clean. It was a 'belt and braces design' like the external security devices layered to catch out the sloppy and based on observation and understanding of how most people's minds work, relying on the lazy mans mantra, 'Why do more than you need to?'

The computer itself was disposable. Whatever information The Grey Man needed or had collected was stored in servers all over the world. Once he moved to a new safe house, all the equipment here would be destroyed and new hardware installed there. He had almost no personal possessions, nothing he had any sentimental affection for. Everything was transient.

The computer allowed him access to an unbelievable world. The Grey Man knew many secrets but this was one of the greatest - Nothing was secure. George Orwell had it almost right. The only people in the world allowed to keep real secrets are the security organisations owned by governments. Everyone else, from ordinary people to large companies, were allowed some level of privacy but to keep the world safe, intelligence organisations needed to be able to override these at any time. Long ago the security services had devised ways to get into computer systems and invented the myth of teenage hackers breaking codes. It was, as usual, smoke and mirrors. Governments of the day needed information, the security services got them this information by systematically controlling and breaking software. Fifty years of development left every computer an open book to the right people. The Grey Man was one of these. Even his own systems were not foolproof nor were the computer systems he set up for The Firm completely safe, but he had devised ways to look for unwelcome visitors.

'Sniffers' of his own design had been cleverly placed throughout his software. These were highly sophisticated programs looking out for people who were trying to hack in and would almost simultaneously shut down the system and locate the hacker without the hacker knowing. Then, one night, they would get a visit from representatives of The Firm. So far the sniffers had not gone off but The Grey Man was constantly upgrading them.

The only computers today that were almost completely safe were the so-called 'billion dollar systems'. They used a master-slave system which worked as two isolated systems. When both the main Computer and Slave computer were off-line, the main computer (master) would send the slave computer a request for information or information to send. It would then sever all lines to the slave system. The slave system would then go on-line, perform the task, set and pick up any requests for information from the system, shut down the internet access and reconnect with the main computer. This meant that the main computer was never actually live on the internet and hence hacker proof. There was no point hacking the slave computer as it had restricted access to the master, constantly joining and breaking off. The system could do this thousands of times per second. It never exposed the main computer to the hacker. A great solution but the hardware and software costs were astronomical.

The Grey Man had only broken this incredible system once by infiltrating the building and attaching a simple relay device thereby reversing the commands so when it thought it was off-line, it was actually live. Even then it was difficult and only hackable for a few minutes. These computers by cost alone were only used by governments.

Apart from these super computers, The Grey Man had free rein across all the other computers in the world. If he had wanted to, he had the ability to bring down governments or if he was crooked, the ability to steal billions.

The Grey Man made himself a cup of tea in the dingy but spotlessly clean kitchen and pulled up a chair in front of the main monitor. He logged into police files and started to research the various gangs operating in London, getting background on the drugs trade, prices, main players etc, looking for anyone big enough to take control, then widened his search looking for ways that people were importing drugs or were extorting small businesses, then entered the customs internet to run similar searches. He saw a few possibilities but nothing concrete. Whoever was running this was discreet. He needed to get closer and could not do that sitting at his console.

He spent another few hours reading reports getting familiar with the drugs trade and then just as his eyes got too strained and one of his headaches came on, he went to bed. Tomorrow would be a long day.

He woke the next morning and dressed in an old, cheap grey suit with a dark raincoat over the top, collar pulled up partially covering his face, flat cap and scuffed, brown shoes. He looked, as always, like a little old nondescript man. Collins had given him some information on other shop keepers who may already be involved so he set off into London, dropping the car at a railway car park and getting the train and underground into town. It was a grey, drizzly day and as he walked from the station, cold started to seep through his clothes. The small shop selling Asian products he was looking for was opposite a smart new café. He went in and had a light breakfast and then endless cups of tea as he sat looking out of the window at the shop. No one bothered him. The waitress almost forgot he was there. As he watched, many people went in and out of the shop but none looked dangerous or the right type. He had been around bad men all his life and would know his quarry. Finally a large Mercedes pulled up outside on the double yellow lines and the passenger got out - a big overweight man in his mid forties wearing a dark coat and displaying a diamond earring and chunky gold bracelet. The man quickly scanned the street for anything amiss and then disappeared into the shop and appeared five minutes later with a parcel bulging out of his coat pocket. The car sped off. 'Not exactly subtle,' thought The Grey Man.

He pulled out his phone, accessed the internet and got onto a special secure website, then punched in the car registration number.

The car's owner and home address was immediately displayed. He entered that into the secure police files and got a string of information about the owner which he sent to his main computer to read later.

From here he took taxis to three other possible receivers registering one more incident. This was almost identical to the earlier one he had observed and involved a shady character entering a shop, his driver remaining outside with the engine running and the man leaving with a parcel. He took down the car number again and repeated the process sending all the information down to the mainframe. He then went to a cheap pub by London Bridge station where he sat quietly in the gloom with the normal afternoon drunks. Being by a station, there were few locals, mainly transit customers so he blended in and nursed a drink for another three hours waiting for darkness to fall.

Once it was dark he contacted The Firm and had another car bought to a place around a thirty minute walk away from the pub. As he walked he followed his normal surveillance pattern ensuring he was not followed and then drove to the first man's address in south London. He waited for an hour but after a no show he drove onto the other address. Here, he found the car he had seen earlier. It was parked in the drive at the side of the house. It was a normal three bedroom house on a modern estate. The houses were crowded together and cars and dogs were everywhere. The place was scruffy like many suburbs of London and not particularly quiet with small gangs of youths on the corner of the streets hanging out.

The Grey Man parked a few hundred yards away, slipped from his car and walked slowly along the pavement putting on an older man's gait and bent posture. A light rain began to fall. At the mark's car he tripped and fell down heavily. A middle-aged black woman saw him fall and helped him to stand asking continuously, "Are you OK, love?" Obviously concerned for the old boy. He smiled his thanks and lent against the car, gathering his strength.

"I will be fine. Thank you," he said in a slurred voice. The woman smiled back, turned and walked down the street. The Grey Man slipped a small device just up and under the back wheel arch of the car. It looked like a tablet and disappeared into the rim. The Grey Man steadied himself then hobbled slowly away.

The tablet was a piece of design that The Grey Man specialised in. It was a unique tracking device. Originally bugs and tracking devices were electrically powered either from the mains for internal use or a battery for mobile use. It did not take long to develop instruments that could detect them, sweeps from a snooper device looking for that tiny electrical current were easily performed and by the early 1960s most conventional electronic tracking devices were made redundant. Then with the advent of microchip technology, a new passive device called a transducer was invented. It had no power source but when radiated by a specific radio frequency would vibrate as it tuned in, the vibrations or resonance generated a small voltage that could be amplified using the new solid state technology and converted back into a radio signal. With no power source to detect, it was invisible to conventional instruments when not in use. The added value was that it would only vibrate to a specific wavelength and was almost impossible to find. Ways to break this device took many years with finer and finer snoopers being designed that could generate these specific wavelengths but it was a very hit and miss affair as highly specific wavelengths were used. Until one bright spark designed a shotgun approach, a snooper that generated powerful signals across the whole spectrum. It swamped all transducers in the vicinity causing them to vibrate along with the strong electrical currents. A sledge hammer to crack a nut. It worked perfectly and within months the security transducer was obsolete, reduced to history. No one swept for these devices anymore and other more sophisticated technologies had now been invented.

This is where The Grey Man had stepped in. He incorporated the new code making properties of 27 bit encryption into a transducer.

Now only a specifically encrypted signal would excite the transducer. Any shotgun approach would not work as it needed a combination frequency broadcast simultaneously, not just a blanket frequency. Like fitting a lock instead of a door latch. A work of sheer brilliance.

He then started to refine the devices, first making them smaller and smaller, then adding contact adhesives with a limited life so the bug fell off after a pre-programmed time. The latest improvement was a bio-degradable version which when finished its work would quickly degrade and wash away. Used throughout The Firm, it was the main tracking device in operation.

Once the tracker was placed he drove back to the farmhouse going through his normal security drills. Inside he activated the computer and started to run a number of software programs. The first was linked to the device and GPS program. It would monitor the car's stop and starts throughout the day. The coordinates of any stop that took less than ten minutes would be sent to another program that would look for small businesses around the immediate area, specifically restaurants and shops that were owned by immigrants.

Once a company was recognised as a likely receiver, a third program would start to gather information on that business, setting up a full data file with the owner's name and full bank and business information, mostly gained from official files. The program also cross referenced this company with any import activities and listed all parcels received in the last six months, from whom and where, to start to isolate the source.

The Grey Man also started a search on the person who owned the car running through all police, tax, credit card and bank information, building a complete picture. 'One down,' thought The Grey Man. 'Now to find your friends.'

Once the programs had done their job, he should be able to map out this gang members area, his likely receivers and also some of the associates that were working with him. This would also give him a pattern of work and a feel for the who and the what, but he really needed all of the gang members. To do this, he had to get inside the network. This would lead to the bosses and a full organisation layout and that meant he had to get close.

As he read the data coming in, he was getting a feel for the type of person he was mapping and gambled that the local pub would feature high in his life.

Twice now The Grey Man had been in the man's vicinity, at the original place where he spotted him and when he placed the transducer. If the man was a professional he would have been seen and under normal surveillance rules he should outsource the next step rather than get close to him again. However, having no one else, he decided it was worth the chance.

Chapter 8

That evening The Grey Man dressed in an old shiny black suit, dirty white shirt and a faded tie, over the top went a soiled, beige, ripped, cheap rain coat and to complete the look chipped broken glasses taped with sticky plaster over one corner topped off by a flat cap. He looked in the mirror and smiled a crooked smile. What reflected back was a scruffy old man best avoided, certainly not someone you would want to talk or mix with - bar flotsam. He poured some scotch down his front and rinsed his teeth with it sloshing the scotch round and spitting into the sink.

He drove to within a mile of the area and walked, slightly unsteadily, to the pub nearest to the man's house. It was a typical London pub, formica table tops and lino floor. A man's pub - dirty, loud and smelly, that even early on a Friday evening was busy. He bought a scotch and settled into a seat in the corner, huddled over, looking down at the table top and as usual was ignored by everyone.

An hour later the mark came in and soon took up at the bar holding court, surrounded by a few hangers on. He was obviously a regular. The Grey Man waited and waited listening to the loud bragging voice echoing round the bar. Finally the man pulled out his mobile phone and made a call. It was exactly what The Grey Man wanted. He pushed a button on a device in his pocket and directed it towards the man. Another one of his inventions activated.

It was a simple device based on common technology as always, called The Link. The device automatically hooked into the man's phone stealing everything stored on it, just as modern cars automatically connect with a mobile and allow hands free operation. However this device, if the phone was in operation, did not allow the person to know he was being linked, the screen only showed information on the call, whilst the device took far more than a car system would.

The phone was unlisted, a pay-as-you-go device which was, of course, not registered to the man, but possessed a wealth of information.

The Grey Man needed ten seconds and counted down slowly as the man talked, oblivious to the fact that he was being hooked. Once the count reached zero, he hit a button on The Link, finished his drink and slipped out the pubs side door. 'Got you,' he whispered.

The Grey Man drove back to the farmhouse elated. 'We are dealing with amateurs,' he thought. 'Thank God.'

He connected The Link to the computer through the USB port and downloaded all the information on it. Up came the phone book with all the addresses and recent activity. He hacked into the network supplier through the accounts department and into the system that showed all the numbers that had been called and received and what each call cost then downloaded the information. Now The Grey Man had every number both called and received since the phone was brought. He activated some new software and sent it off looking for those numbers, finding the phones and who they were registered to and their addresses. The phones, that were unregistered and pay-as-you-go, he crossed reference to billings. As most top-ups were paid for by credit card, The Grey Man could easily find all their personal information from the credit card companies.

Once he received this information he activated a program called The Net. A very complicated system which looked at all those phones calls not only from the mark but all the other telephone numbers he now had. It looked at all the sent and received calls from the now huge number of calls, and cross referenced each one to find out who knew who. Expanding the contacts, Than set up a system that linked into the giant security computer at GCHQ which specialised in government level snooping and set up an electronic recording program (ERP). All calls made from these phones and received would now be recorded. The Grey Man finally set up the menu to look for specific key buzzwords which he hoped the villains would use at their work; words such as pickup, drop off, and all common slang words for drugs. He would study these calls later as he filtered out the information that was unnecessary, the daily dross of people's lives.

Once this was underway he looked closely at the marks phone especially the telephone numbers that had been called and received the most, surmising they would be, the most likely to be involved. He retrieved their names and addresses and started the earlier software program of investigating the owners looking for police records, credit cards, tax, bank information.

Altogether there was a vast hydra of information everything he would need. Who, what, and where, and even though most of the investigating was automated, replacing what would have been a huge team, it would still take days and weeks of sifting and co-ordinating to get a picture to emerge, something The Grey Man excelled in. By the end of it he would know everyone in the organisation and almost everything about them.

Chapter 9

Surge could not find sleep, his mind returning again and again to his early years, thinking about the big change and the little man.

After two years the borstal had a new governor, an older man, semi-retired, ex-military who bought with him a strength and sense of purpose. On his second day looking from the window into the exercise yard, noticed Surge, stripped to the waist. He was amazingly muscled for one so young with a true V figure, wide powerful shoulders and big arms, down to a six pack stomach and small waist. He was doing a strange crab like jump twist dance looking almost demented. There was no music playing and he was not wearing earphones. The new governor watched for a while. It looked so familiar but odd, some of the steps he was sure he knew. Then it clicked and he sent for Surge's file. The governor had recognised many of the moves from his time in special forces.

The dance was something Surge had invented. He was not allowed to outwardly practise the martial arts in borstal so instead used the weight training room to build his strength and the yard to covertly exercise his fighting skills, by modifying the normal katas which are present in so many different styles. In the exercise yard he went through technique after technique sometimes with his eyes closed, imagining fighting multiple opponents, placing his foot just right, lifting a knee, spinning but without throwing a kick or punch or strike. He ignored the final piece which would give the game away. It was enough to be in the right place at the right time. He worked out where an opponent would strike, moving his body, head, wrist, arm, shoulder, etc, to avoid any potential blows and then counter striking but never actually finishing the move off. Once in position and ready, in his mind, and only in his mind, throw the punch kick or strike, then work out where that body would fall, avoiding it and looking for the next opponent and move again. Because the attack was never finished it looked from the outside just like a weird set of movements without rhyme or reason, very fast jumping, crouching, twisting, spinning, sometimes back flips or forward rolls, dropping to the floor and flipping back to his feet, almost balletic, incredibly athletic but very strange to watch.

Over the two years inside, Surge had gone through every technique he had ever been taught and was now inventing new ones to keep himself alive and fit.

The new governor made a call to a special number and was passed through department after department, many not supposed to exist. Finally he talked to a man he had only heard of as a rumour, one of the top spooks. The man listened quietly as the governor told Surge's story and described the dance. Then asked a couple of pertinent questions about Surge's character; Was he a good mixer? Did he have any special friends? How intelligent was he? and finally said, "Leave it with me. I will be in touch shortly" before hanging up.

Three days later a small wiry man around forty with short hair and a thin moustache, turned up at the borstal. He wore green army loose fitting combat trousers, a white shirt with open collar, regulation plimsolls and held a neat but used sports bag. He looked compact, smart and very fit, ramrod straight with powerful arms, a barrel chest and small waist.

The governor called Surge to the gym and the little man sat at a desk asking Surge to sit in a chair opposite. Once Surge had sat down the stranger turned to the governor and asked him to leave and to ensure no one came in. It was done quietly but with authority. There was no doubt who was in charge. The little man took from his sports bag a file with Surge's name on it and went through the facts of Surge's life in a clipped authoritarian style. He had a strong voice with a trace of a cockney accent. He initially named dates and places, Surge's birth, school, father, mother's name, the arrest and time in borstal, just focusing on the facts until he came to the martial arts. He then stopped and looked Surge directly in the eye and asked him how good he thought he was. Surge replied he was OK.

"Let's see," said the little man and stood up removing his shirt to show a white PT vest underneath. Surge just sat there.

"Get up," said the man.

"No," said Surge. "If I hit you I will get into serious trouble."

The little man bent forward, stared Surge in the eye and from six inches away shouted in his best parade voice,

"If you do not fucking get up, I am going to beat the shit out of you, you little bastard. Get up NOW and defend yourself!"

Surge stood and the little man attacked two roundhouse punches left and right easily blocked by Surge, who then felt a sharp pain in the kidneys. The two punches were feints. The little man smiled. "Let's try again," he said.

Surge assumed his fighting stance then circled and stepped in throwing kicks and punches. The little man blocked and moved, moving beautifully always in balance and Surge was amazed at his style and smoothness. No question he was an expert. Surge increased the speed of his attacks going up a gear as did the little man keeping pace with Surge effortlessly, punches and kicks landed on both men but they ignored them.

Surge revelled in the combat. He did not have to hold anything back. This man could cope. Surge freed his mind and body, going up yet another gear. It was a superb dance, both men in harmony and balance, faster and more deadly with each minute. Surge saw techniques of attack that he marvelled at, sending his mind spinning in new directions that he would explore later. He knew he was bigger, younger and stronger than the little man but was amazed what he could do. Time and again the little man blocked, moved and spun away, attacking from impossible angles with a precision and control Surge had never seen before and Surge met him every step of the way. Then Surge saw sweat start on the little man's brow. It ran down his face and into his eyes. He felt rather than saw an imperceptible slowing down as the smaller, older man started to tire and Surge brought it down back under control. With that the little man stepped back, stood straight then brought his arms up to his chest and formally bowed. Surge bowed back. "Outstanding," was all he said.

They both sat down, the little man gathering his breath. Surge was hardly breathing at all.

After a second he said, "What do you want to do when you are free?"

"I have no idea," replied Surge. "Who would want a boy from a borstal?"

The little man smiled for the second time that day.

"Well," he said. "I work for the British Government in a special department that helps national security. We safeguard the country allowing ordinary men and woman to get on with their lives. We do jobs other men cannot do."

It was obviously a well worn rehearsed script but Surge lent forward anyway.

"My job is to look for eagles like you. Men who stand alone, are strong, independent resourceful and brave. Men who can protect the doves. Would you be interested?"

"What are you offering?" said Surge.

The little man went quiet then said, "I offer you pain, loneliness, fear and paranoia, a lifetime of looking over your shoulder to see your enemy who one day will come and break your back, make no mistake. You will do and see things that will sear your brain and harden your heart and at the end a small pension and a warning that if you ever speak of it, the Official Secrets Act will lock you up and will throw away the key."

Without hesitation Surge said "When do I start?".

"Now," said the man, not at all surprised. "Follow me." With that they walked back to the dorm where Surge collected what possessions he had. Then calmly they both walked out the door through the gates, past the guards and into a small car and drove away into the night.

Surge broke off from the memories. He finally lay back on the bed turned over and slept. Tomorrow was going to be a new day. For the first time in a long time he had purpose and direction but the doubts surfaced. Did he have the legs to finish the race? Only time would tell.

Chapter 10

Collins sat through the funeral in a kind of daze. The normal friends, family and well-wishers attended and he moved through the day on autopilot. He had learnt long ago how to hide his emotions in public and presented a distant, stoic persona, not so Jon, an only child who had been brought up with a mostly absent father. He had been very close to his mother. Her death had hit him hard, and as they sat there in the pew side by side, Collins reached out and put his arm round him and Jon sobbed for both of them.

That evening Collins sat on his marriage bed and looked at the room which was full of his wife's life, pictures of holidays, their wedding and Jon growing up were framed on every cabinet and on the walls, wonderful days. Even her perfume lingered in the air. After a while he went to the drawer at the bottom of the wardrobe and pulled it out and onto the bed. His wife had nagged him for years that were anything to happen to her all the information he would need would be there. The drawer was full, everything neat and tidy as was her way. At the top were some old photos of them as youngsters, when they had first met. One made his breath catch in his throat. She was about twenty years old, wearing combat fatigues which rather than detracted actually emphasised her femininity, the belt pulled tight to her tiny waist. She had an AK47 slung casually over her arm and her face and hair shone with a glow only an Israeli sun can give. Bright blue eyes. He had forgotten quite how wonderful she used to look. He stared at it for some time then put it aside. Next was a typed list of instructions explaining which insurance company they were with, how to pay gas, electricity bills, milkman, bank details, credit card numbers, etc. It very carefully spelt out all the things she did in running the house. She knew he would not know where to start and for some reason the list touched him greatly. How well she knew him.

Lastly there was a letter which he opened slowly.
Dearest Husband

If you are reading this then I have gone before you which was always my wish. I cannot tell you how much I love you and how walking through life with you has been such a pleasure. I could not have asked for anything more. Look after Jon. He was your greatest gift to me and ensure that he knows nothing of our past. Let him lead a normal life without terror and violence. Keep him safe.

Do not grieve for me my darling for I know we will be reunited again.

Keep safe love,

Your Loving Wife

He struggled to read the last line as the tears ran down his face and dripped from the tip of his nose smudging the ink. He felt an overwhelming wave of emotion, terrible grief which threatened to sweep him away. Downstairs was a case full of guns and part of him wanted to go down there, pull one out and kill himself but he had two reasons not to. The first was his son Jon who he loved more than life. The second was his own and his race's call for vengeance, not justice, but hard and bloody vengeance. His whole life had been about fighting, first for his country's birth where the world learnt what it meant to be an Israeli, then for his government and now for his wife.

Fury overcame the grief and for a second became again, the man he used to be. Someone he had tried to lock away to put behind him as he led a normal life. A man feared for decades, a cold blooded Assassin who swore on everything he believed in that the person responsible would die.

Next morning he met Jon for breakfast in their large kitchen diner. Neither of them had any idea where anything was. Collins had never made a meal in the twenty years they had lived there. This was his wife's domain. Jon was the loved son of a Jewish mother who doted on him. Collins opened and closed cupboards finally finding what he needed and knocked up some eggs and toast. He realised then he had better make a shopping list and get items from the shop or they would starve, something else new to him.

"What's next for me?" said Jon when they had settled down.

"University," said Collins, watching his son's face fall. "Two reasons. One your Mother would have wanted and expected you to get your degree and two, we will be watched to see if anything has changed. They will want to know if we are going to the police or maybe trying something on our own. We must show normality. It must look to them as though we have accepted the situation and so put them at their ease. Once that happens, we smoke them out and deal with them."

"How dad? said Jon. "I know you had a military past but this is different. How can you and your two friends take on organised crime?"

"Let me tell you a little of my past that we have kept away from you," said Collins. "I was born, as was your mother, in troubled times. I did not have the kind of upbringing you have had. Israel had only come into existence a handful of years earlier and we were surrounded by enemies. I had to fight for my country like most young men of my time. From a very early age we all went to war. Most men did their time in the forces and then went onto a normal life but I was different. I found I had a talent for violence. Weapons came easy to me. I loved my country. I loved the army and I had a skill. I could shoot any gun placed in my hand accurately straight off. I could move quietly and had an aptitude for hand to hand combat, difficult to see in your old man now but when I was younger I was dangerous and full of anger. First I joined the army, then I was seconded into special operations mainly behind enemy lines. Unlike most men I was very good at killing . As I grew older my skills became honed and I became a spook ,a spy, specialising in assassination, working initially for my government and later friendly nations, going after anyone who would attack my country or its friends. I was not a mercenary. I only did what I did to protect and preserve."

"During this time I met The Grey Man. Who was an intelligence specialist. The best. He would help me plan difficult operations. Where the information came from I will never know. He was a legend even then. Later I met Surge who ran interference for me, taking out anyone who was between me and my target. You should have seen him, Jon. He was truly awesome."

"Also during this time I met and fell in love with your mother. She knew what I did and still loved me. However she would not become part of that world, insisting we move to England and start a new life where we could bring you up in anonymity and relative safety. I agreed and we brought this house and I set up my import export business, became freelance working for governments and The Firm mainly training and coaching."

"What is The Firm?" asked Jon.

"A secret that can wait for another day," said Collins. "The point of telling you my story is this. I am not just a storekeeper. The Grey Man is not just old and Surge is not just a fat drunk. We are professionals with a lifetime of experience beyond your imaginings. Trust me and do exactly what any of us say to you and I promise you this will end up right."

"Now for you the plan is to go back to uni, focus on your studies and forget anything else. In three months I will come for you and will explain exactly what will happen next and your place in it. Is this OK?"

"Sure," said Jon.

"The last thing," said Collins. "Is that you must never speak to anyone about this or anything else I trust you with. Not a girlfriend or your best pal. When I say to you that our lives depend on your silence I am not exaggerating."

"I promise dad. Not a word to a soul."

Collins ruffled his son's head. "This is very difficult for you, I know. Your world has been turned upside down. Stay with me son. Your blood is my blood and this is our way."

The rest of the morning was melancholy for Collins. Letting insurance companies and the rates and the gas board and electricity companies know that his wife had died and he was now the main person to contact, going over and over the same story. Telling complete strangers was hard but had to be done.

Finally he went to the bank. He had to close her account and transfer what little there was to his account. At the bank he was met by the young smartly dressed bank manager who showed him into a private office. He had heard of the tragedy and offered his condolences.

"Did your wife know something was going to happen to her?" asked the manager.

"No. I don't think," so said Collins. "Why do you ask?"

"A few years ago she asked for a meeting," said the manager. "She explained that one day soon she might die and left me detailed information about all her financial dealings for your pension."

Collins gave a wry smile. "My wife was from Israel," he said. "All Israeli women think that they will not last. They are all fatalists. It is part of their culture."

"Oh," said the manager. "I did wonder." And he passed across a large brown envelope. "Everything your wife has saved is detailed there and her investments in her portfolio."

"I am sure it is fine," said Collins. "I need some running money and wonder if you could cash in everything she has."

The bank manager looked aghast. "It is rather a lot of money," he said.

Collins smiled. "My wife ran a small corner shop not Marks & Spencer. What can she have? A few thousand at most."

It was time for the bank manager to smile. "Your wife was a little cleverer than that. Investing wisely in stocks and bonds."

He slid across a slip of paper. "This is what she has accumulated." On the paper was written in a clear hand £123,000. Collins was amazed. His wife had never mentioned any nest egg but he thought back. She never wanted to spend money no matter how much he earned, always clever and frugal planning for a rainy day. He thought how well he knew his wife and ultimately how little he knew about her. How could she have saved all this money and never a word he wondered? He arranged for the transfer of everything into his own account, thanked the manager and left, feeling somehow better and worse than when he walked in.

Collins had put it off long enough but finally drove to the little corner store which his wife had run and where she had been killed. It was situated next to a fish and chip shop, laundrette and take away Chinese restaurant, at the edge of a large council estate just back from the main road with parking to the front. The front door was right at the corner of the block, painted a dark blue and windows stretched down both roads. It had been chosen because it was within walking distance of Jon's school.

He stood outside for a while. This was his wife's domain. In the twenty years they had owned it he had hardly been inside. When they moved to England and he was still constantly travelling, she had insisted on having something to do so he had bought her the shop and she had made it clear from day one he was not welcome in the running or managing of her business. She would work here during the day and Jon would go there straight from school normally with a few friends to play in the flat above. At 5.30pm on the dot the friends would go home and he would be given his tea made on the old stove in the tiny kitchen. She would then continue serving in the shop and Jon would do his homework and watch TV until Collins came to pick them up at 9.00pm to take them home, or if he was travelling the taxi would arrive.

Jon would go to bed and Collins and his wife would eat a late supper before retiring. The next morning at 8.00 am if Collins was working in England, he would drive them back to the shop to start another day.

On Saturdays, Jon worked in the shop all day helping his mother and earning his pocket money. It was an unusual life but it worked. Both Collins and his wife had their own freedom inside a secure marriage. Now all that had come to an end.

Collins found the keys. He unlocked the shop and went inside. Nothing had changed. It had been five days since the murder and the shop looked as pristine as ever. Collins was touched that all the blood had been cleaned up and everything was back in its place as if nothing had happened. The store was shelved on all walls with a centre section running the length of the shop dividing it into two aisles. At the end was the dairy food in the chilled cabinet. The rest were filled with an assortment of tins and boxes which made up a normal corner shop.

Collins took out his phone and called a distant cousin whose son Eli worked for his wife. He told Eli that he was reopening for business and asked him to come round, thanking him for cleaning up and explaining that he would pay him for the five day's lost salary with the shop being closed. As he waited he walked up and down the aisles familiarising himself with the goods and prices. 'How do you run a shop?' he wondered.

Finally Eli turned up and explained to Collins the daily rituals of till and stock taking and reordering. Upstairs Collins found an old brown apron which he put on and set to work. They cleared out anything that was past the sell-by date. Eli picked up the phone and talked directly to all the suppliers explaining that Collins was taking over and it was business as usual placing replacement orders. All were happy to hear the business would continue.

Customers started to come through the door greeting Eli and introducing themselves to Collins. Many gave commiserations. Many stopped to chat. The place acted like a coffee shop and the aisles were often full of neighbours standing and talking. It seemed the norm and Collins did little to stop it. At first he play acted the little storekeeper, being polite and friendly and then much to his surprise found he was enjoying himself, being dragged into the community and the gossip.

On the third day, just as he felt he was slotting into his new role, a young woman came into the shop, a baby in a pram and a toddler clinging to her hand. She wore threadbare clothes, an old pair of jeans and faded tee-shirt with worn down shoes which although they had seen better days were clean. The children he noticed were much better turned out than she was with the blanket inside the old pram looking new. She wandered around the aisles looking but not touching anything waiting for the shop to empty, then went to the till and asked to have a private word with Collins. He walked her to the back of the shop and she started to talk in a hesitant way. "Your wife and I used to have an arrangement. If I ran short, she would let me have a few things on tick. Is that still OK?" she asked.

Collins looked at her hard and thought, 'Why not? What do I care?'

"Sure," he said "Go ahead."

She took a basket and put a few things into it. Baby food, wipes, nappies etc. He noticed nothing for herself. She took them to the till and Collins started to transfer the goods from the basket into the plastic bag. She stopped him. "You have to put them through the till and give me the receipt." she said.

"Fine" said Collins, happy to play the game.

She thanked him and left and he wiped the incident from his mind. 'Charity is good for the soul', he thought.

The next day she was back basket now in hand. She filled it to the top with goods. Collins, although a rich man, was a little miffed. He was happy to extend a little charity but this girl he thought was pushing it. She finally went to the till and he again started to bag the goods.

"Through the till please" said the girl. Collins huffed and puffed a bit. She was coming on a bit strong, he thought. He again rung up the goods and passed the girl the till receipt. Much to his surprise, she pulled out an old faded purse and started to count out the money owed, putting the receipt from the day before next to the new one on the counter. She paid in full then looked Collins right in the eye, and said quietly, politely but with some force, "Sometimes my giro gets delayed. Now I had a business arrangement with your wife which I would like to continue with you if that's OK but I do not need or want your charity. Do you understand?"

Collins was a bit taken aback looking at this serious, strong, young woman. Finally he said, "Whatever arrangement you had with my wife still stands," and he reached out his right hand. She shook it solemnly.

"Thank you," she said storing the goods below the pram on a small wire ledge. Collins walked round the counter and opened the door. Both smiled and he saw how pretty and how young she was. He stood for a while gazing after her as she walked away, old faded pram in front, toddler tucked under her arm, wondering what life she was leading, amazed at her dignity, overcoming the embarrassment of poverty. Somehow it cheered him for the rest of the day.

Over the next few days as he familiarised himself with the shop getting deliveries, balancing the till and stocking shelves amazed at numerous examples of a helping community. The number of people buying for neighbours and friends and the number of deliveries Eli made to people who could not manage to get out, on his old fashioned bicycle complete with front basket. In this way the old, infirm and ill were catered for. He soon realised, how much of a hub of the community the shop was and how many depended on its service. So many people who could not afford the bus fare to go to the huge hypermarkets or did not have the energy to lug their shopping home. So many people just needing a small financial sub during the week to get them through to their pension or giro. Unemployment was high in this area especially amongst the middle aged and old. Many struggled to make ends meet. The shop met many of their needs. Collins had travelled the world trying to "right rights" but realised his wife had probably done more good in this little shop then he ever had.

Every day that he worked he waited, knowing contact would come. The villains had set the scene and would now want to follow through. Collins had not made a fuss and they would read that he did not want to come under police scrutiny, perhaps had something to hide. It at least made him vulnerable in their eyes and he knew they would return. He hoped when they came he was strong enough to keep the facade up. He knew he could kill any who came against him but did not want the soldiers, he wanted the top man the one who gave the orders and then he wanted to smash the organisation that preyed on the weak. Ten days in the contact came.

Smith sat in his car. It was the third day in a row he had sat here just watching the shop front seeing the little Jewish shopkeeper go in and out checking for anything out of the ordinary where the police may have been alerted. If he had it would be unusual. Most immigrants wanted no trouble, no way to bring themselves to the attention of the government officials. Almost all had the correct documentation but knew that these could be withdrawn at any moment. Any noise or fuss could bring down trouble.

This was the part of the job he loved. Lee had outsourced everything else. All pickups, cutting and distribution were all done by local gangs but the recruitment and subsequent intimidation and blackmail had to be kept close. Smith was well pleased. He had always enjoyed beating and scaring weaker men. A big man himself he loved to see the fear come into a victim's eyes when he came near them. This one would be no different. Just before closing and when the assistant had left, Smith checked that the shop was empty and stepped inside, quickly turning and locking the deadbolt and reversing the open sign. He then walked to the back of the shop opened a small cupboard and switched off the mains electricity. He had done his homework. The lights all went out as did the solitary CCTV camera based above the counter.

The little Jew came bustling down the shop spluttering, "What are you doing? What are you doing?"

Smith casually backhanded him across the face knocking him to the floor before giving him two well placed kicks in the ribs. The storekeeper lay there floundering, tears in his eyes. "Why are you doing this?" he begged.

Smith bent down, grabbed him by the shirt front and lifted him one handed until their faces almost touched. "Your wife owed me a lot of money," he said.

"For what?" said the shopkeeper.

"For me to look after her. I now want my payment"

"Why should I pay?" said the old man.

"Because you have a son that could go the same way as your wife but maybe a little slower and a bit more painfully. Do we understand each other?" Smith was loving this.

The storekeeper was almost in floods of tears. "How much?" he whispered.

"£500 per week, collected by a friend," replied Smith.

"But I cannot pay that. It is only a small shop."

"Well," said Smith. "Pay me for a few weeks and maybe there could be a small service you can do me to lessen the bill. Do you understand?" Spittle from Smith's mouth was flecking the storekeeper's face.

"Sure, sure, I do not want any more trouble," he cried.

"OK," said Smith. "Used notes, Friday. A man will come here and say he is from Smith. Pay him. And one more thing. If you go to the police I promise you no shop, no son, no life. Are we clear?"

The shopkeeper nodded, as they all did. Smith stepped in and just for the fun of it punched him in the stomach and then again in the face knocking him to the floor. "Just so you do," he said and walked out.

Collins lay on the floor. Everything screamed at him to kill the bastard and he knew he could. There was enough stuff in the shop to use as a weapon and he had got close enough to take him out with his bare hands. Tears had fallen from his eyes in frustration. His body and blood called out for the kill but he kept himself under iron control. He wanted the man giving the orders not the soldiers and he wanted to smash the organisation.

He stood up brushing the dust from his clothes. He watched the man from the window and then whispered, "You are dead. Fucking dead!" He turned round and kicked a magazine stand so hard it shot down the aisle, magazines everywhere. He stopped, stood perfectly still then took a few deep breaths. Having controlled himself, he then carefully righted the stand and got down on his hands and knees picking all the magazines up and putting them back in place. He had seen the enemy and would destroy them.

Chapter 11

Surge sat at the kitchen table thinking the problems through, deciding how he could get fit. Previously all that was needed was to work his body hard knowing that it would respond, but now in his fifties had to be careful. At 20 or even as late as 40 he would have donned running shoes and run until the fat burned off but things today were different. This old body simply would not tolerate that kind of abuse. He had not checked but guessed that his blood pressure would be high due to his recent lifestyle and any over enthusiastic exercise could see a fatal heart attack or stroke. In some respects even a torn muscle or strain would see him out of this game for now, in middle age, it took him weeks and months to recover after almost any injury.

A slow steady approach he felt was the only way, working each part of his body in a rotation system. As one part grew tired a short rest then move on to the next. He would also go on a low fat, low carb, high protein diet.

Surge had arrived at the flat with nothing but the clothes he stood up in, the high tech phone from The Grey Man and money. Time to stock up, then get working he thought. The flat was based in an old council style block next to five other equally ugly blocks built in the 1960's. Most had been sold during Thatcher's era and since then had been better maintained by the residents, even though this still remained a tough working class area. The nearest shopping centre was a mile away with a row of small family owned shops topped off by a new large supermarket which sold everything they did but cheaper and was gradually putting them all out of business. He went there first. In the clothing aisle Surge bought underwear, socks, jeans, trousers, T-shirts, jumpers and a sweatshirt with a hood. From there he worked his way to the food department first buying green tea, which he would live on, as apart from water, that would be his only liquid intake, then running through all the foodstuffs he wanted only choosing low saturated fats and low in sugar foods. He had always eaten well and the fat around his middle was mainly due to the thousands of pints of beer he had drunk. However, if he was going to exercise he needed to ensure he had plenty of energy and bought fresh vegetables fish and meat plus a few potatoes to ensure some carbohydrate intake, then lots of soup packets and tins of soup, an old dieting trick he had learned way back. The body digests food and liquid quickly and easily but soup was more difficult, it stayed in your system for longer and released the energy slower making you feel less hungry. Lastly he bought some toiletries.

At the till he picked up some sturdy 'bags for life' and packed both full. They were quite heavy and as he walked back to the flat he lifted them one at a time every five steps to his chest and back down again. Anyone watching would have laughed at the comical sight. Back at the flat he made a hot green tea which he drunk as he went through the cupboards looking for appliances. He finally found what he was looking for. A blender and juicer. There was normally one hidden in a cupboard in these safe houses as they looked a good idea when bought but hardly anyone actually used them. He stripped to his pants and went through a series of callisthenics. First stretching, then squats, press ups and sit ups, finally finishing with martial art style punches and kicks, moving his body around the front room in a curious dance, imagining opponents and dealing with them. The sweat flowed after a few minutes and he felt tired but overall had done better than expected. His body appearing to be OK so far with the pressure he was forcing on it.

Surge showered, dressed in his new clothes and went back to the high street, this time going to a camping outdoor shop. Here he spent some time looking for a rucksack, finally with the eye of an expert, buying one of the most expensive which fitted him well. He then bought a two man tent with built in groundsheet, trousers and waterproof jacket of a high quality this allowed the material to breathe as he walked, a water bottle, some good quality socks, a compass and series of ordnance survey maps, finally spending the most time and money on the softest leather walking boots in the shop. All was packed into the rucksack which Surge slung on, adjusting the straps to accommodate the weight and then walked back to the flat. There he made himself a meal of tuna, raw eggs, sweet corn and milk all blended together in a smoothie, pulled on his walking socks and boots, hooded sweatshirt, half filled the rucksack with tins and went for a walk. With the rain gently falling down, his body almost immediately went into a rhythmic mode. How many thousands of miles had he walked on route marches, he wondered, letting his mind wander but after only about an hour, to his annoyance, started to feel weary, strange pains appeared in his knees, hips and feet, his body complaining of the use after so many years of inaction. Also the small of his back and in between his shoulder blades were aching and the rucksack rubbed his hips. He stopped, took off the rucksack and went through some more stretching, put the backpack back on and readjusted the straps gritted his teeth and kept walking. Finally he gained his second wind, his body responded and started to warm up, moving more easily and Surge allowed his mind to drift as the miles rolled by.

He thought of the first time he had met The Grey Man. It was the late 70s. By then Surge was running a small team of US rangers and SAS rotating from their individual regiments. His spook work was seen as good training for them. They were doing odd jobs from burglary, laying bugs to kidnapping and intimidation, all to people from foreign hostile countries who were overstepping the mark in the UK. At that time, football hooliganism had reached an all time high with rival gang leaders now working together using telephones to organise fights in stadiums and in town centres up and down the country. The government of the day thought it an outrage and the general public were getting fed up, starting to boycott the national game. Surge was delegated to bring it to a stop and The Grey Man was seconded to help.

The very first time they met, face to face, was in a small office in the centre of London. Surge and his team arrived early and sat around the bare formica table. The Grey Man arrived five minutes later, set up a flipchart and proceeded to lecture as if this was a sales or management meeting in a small company, all graphs, photos and facts. At that time he was dressed in a smart blue suit, white shirt, blue tie, small, brown glasses and neatly combed short cut brown hair. He looked like middle management and would have received not a second glance in the city. Surge never forgot that lecture or the ones that came later, the detail was incredible. There was nothing The Grey Man did not know about their opponents - friends, family, bank details, main habits etc.

The 'mark' he lectured on that day was a thoroughly nasty piece of work, who ran a small successful building firm employing bricklayers, plasterers etc. He had no skills of his own but laboured for his more skilled staff. A large powerful fit man he had made an oversize hod to carry a huge amount of bricks which he ran across the sites forcing his bricklayers into faster work. Their work was ultimately shoddy but no customers complained due to his reputation.

His passion on and off the building site was street fighting, beating up anyone who stood in his way. He had no real interest in football but it gave him a reason to run riot and he had quickly made it to the top, running a very nasty gang. Over the last few years, contacts had been made with rival gangs guaranteeing fun-filled Saturdays of blood and mayhem.

The Grey Man explained in incredible detail about this 'mark' from bank account number to police convictions, wife, friends and acquaintances, even medical details showing broken bones and points of weakness, left or right hand bias, favoured weapons and martial art skills etc. The final part was based around details of fights and up and coming appointments.

The operation was planned in detail for the following Saturday. The object was to neutralise him.

Surge remembered standing on the terraces that cold winters afternoon, the wind whistling from the north and a light rain falling, the smell of hot dogs and the cries of the fans singing their football chants. He stood alone watching the mark with his entourage all around him, shouting and screaming and swearing at the opposing fans. At exactly the time The Grey Man predicted, the riot started. The fence between the warring fans was torn down and they charged each other. Unbeknown to them, all cameras recording the game were under strict instructions not to follow the riot and to concentrate on the game allowing Surge to do his work.

Surge moved smoothly forward and piled into the thick of it with one SAS and one Ranger each side clearing space, dropping thug after thug becoming a wedge with Surge at the point. As he reached the mark, who was on the terrace step just below and behind him, Surge dropped and punched him powerfully with his full weight behind the blow, low into the thugs back cracking the spine and breaking a disk. As the mark fell with the impact and the pain, Surge swung his elbow through an over arm arc and shattered his collar bone. The mark screamed but it was lost in the noise and rage of the melee and he lay on the floor writhing in agony, half conscious, while the battle carried on around him. Just two strikes, made in the blink of an eye in the middle of anarchy unnoticed by anyone else, was all it took and the job was done.

Surge and his team broke off, split up and disappeared. Surge knew the mark would be a changed man. His back would be weakened and for the rest of his life he would walk with a stoop and be in constant pain. The collar bone would never heal properly and tolerate no weight put upon it thereby making the right arm next to useless he felt no remorse no hint of empathy. Live by the sword, die by the sword he thought.

Six more times they repeated the exercise up and down the country before word got out to the thugs that a team was working the leaders of the gangs. Football violence halved then halved again, before it was able to be kept under control by the local police. In all the operation had been a great success and had started off the friendship he had, as much as you were a friend, with The Grey Man.

That night after a long walk Surge got home exhausted. He had a quick supper of steak and roasted vegetables with more green tea then a hot bath. He set the alarm for 6.00am and fell into a deep sleep.

The next morning started off with a light breakfast, a set of callisthenics, stretching and his martial dance. He put some antiseptic cream on his feet and hips where the rubbing had began and set off. He walked until lunchtime through the streets of London, a quick march, head up, back straight, military step speeding through the miles until, too soon for his liking, fatigue set in but he pushed on trying to get in as many miles as possible. Finally tired Surge found an old cafe and ordered scrambled eggs and beans and a glass of water. He ate slowly putting down the cutlery between each mouthful and chewing thoroughly, making his body feel there was more food on the plate then there actually was and sat still allowing his body to rest. He then, at a slower pace, retraced his steps though the dark afternoon's gloom back to the apartment. More stretching and press-ups and sit ups and finally, after going through an old karate kata which he remembered from his youth, lay back on his bed his body aching and tired and read a book that had been left by a previous occupant of the flat until falling into an exhausted sleep.

The next day he took stock. Blisters on both feet not too bad, but more worryingly pains in his right ankle, left knee and lower back. All had been broken five years previously and at the time Surge was told that arthritis would follow. He decided though he could bear the pain and went through the morning exercise ritual and then to a local swimming bath where he slowly swam fifty lengths, stretching his body especially his tired back and leg muscles. Afterwards he felt much better and took a long shower in steaming water before dressing and walking briskly home, found his rucksack and boots and walked all afternoon.

These days started a pattern - two days hard walking, then swim and light walking on the next day, then three days hard walking and then an easier day. Each morning and evening a set of exercises to work his arms stomach and chest muscles. Every day he pushed himself as far as he dared feeling for rips and tears in his overworked muscles.

On the seventh day bone tired Surge rested, just doing chores, shopping, cleaning and visiting charity shops ,buying books and an odd set of clothes. He did not wear these, just washed folded them carefully and put them away. These would be the clothes he wore on operations to be used once and discarded.

At the end of the third week he felt stronger. Drinking no alcohol had changed him and the endorphin lifts from the exercise bought him a feeling of well being. The blisters had healed as they always did and the rucksack full of tins now and much heavier, felt part of his body and no real weight. The last few days Surge had started to change the pace and now loped along in a half jog, half walk movement. It ate up the miles. He decided he needed a test and took a train up to Edale in the Midlands. This was the start of the Pennine Walk, 312 miles along the spine of Britain. It is a tough course but there are many stops along the way and if he was not up to it knew where he could take a break.

The next day Surge left the station and smelt the clean air looking at the rugged hills in front of him and the well worn path disappearing into the distance. England at its most beautiful. The rucksack was now full of his camping equipment with a couple of house bricks at the bottom to push him along. The weather was damp and cool, just the way he liked it and he walked and loped along as the terrain let him. By now his body was responding to the pressure he was putting on it. A lifetime of training had conditioned him and even five years of abuse could not take away that underlying fitness. The only worries were with his joints which constantly complained. His hands were very susceptible to cold so he wore gloves constantly. Both his knee and ankle he strapped which helped. The pain in his back he could do nothing else but ignore stretching before and after each stop.

Lunch time on the first day Surge sat on a large rock looking at a valley stretching away in front of him, clear blue skies and a low wind blowing through the smell of the heather and grass making him feel young again. He opened a cold tin of tomato soup and munched on some granary biscuits as he thought about Collins, a strange man almost schizophrenic. On the one hand a gentle soul who loved his country and was devoted to his family, a man of passion with a big heart, and on the other the cold killer who could use any weapon with astonishing skill and did not blink when he pulled the trigger.

The first time he heard of him was from a group of special forces who he was training at an army camp in the Brecon beacons on what was laughingly called a self defence course. It was where Surge taught his speciality how to break other men. They were all tough soldiers, very experienced with years of training behind them. All thought they could handle themselves. One left the course with a broken wrist, another with a broken rib. All left with a different attitude.

When they had arrived they were full of Collins. He was teaching them how to enter the killing house. This was a series of rooms inside a square building, which had hidden targets in each room. The idea was to go through the house, avoiding the dummy hostages and take out the targets. It was standard stuff with live ammo. Every one of them had had years of practice using the killing house. They had always been trained to be careful, thorough and accurate. Collins was to train them how to be fast.

He sent them in one after another, timing them and then reviewing their speed versus accuracy. Most scored 100% when they went slowly as trained but as they started to speed up they started to miss. Collins discussed each visit and advised ways to improve. At the end of the first morning he went in himself giving the stopwatch to the youngest guy. He halved their fastest time, hitting all targets.

They were, however, unimpressed accusing him of using special target pistols and of course, he knew where the targets were in advance as he had laid the house out. Collins had smiled, put down his pistols and took two from them, the heaviest and bulkiest and smallest and lightest. He then challenged them to each take a room and rearrange the target, then stay inside and watch how he performed.

Being special forces and up for most things they all stood in the most difficult places and for a laugh placed the targets on their heads or held them close to their bodies, anything to make the shot harder and slow Collins down.

They said later that he went through each room at a cross between a walk and a run, not stopping, instantly spotting the target and almost without aiming, fired. He hit every target and reduced his original time by 30% - a stunning performance.

But the main thing that had struck them was his icy coolness. They had held the targets close to their bodies which should have given him pause, would have given any normal man a cause for concern, but the impression he gave them was of apathy, that if he would have missed and shot them, he would not have cared at all. They were unimportant. Hitting the targets was his focus. Even for battle hardened veterans they found this level of callousness unnerving.

They had spent the rest of the week trying to copy his technique, going through the drill thousands of times. All improved but not one got close to his original time. They said he was not human, and spoke of him in awe. After hearing this, Surge had looked him up and that had started the friendship.

The walk was glorious, a feast for the eye and spirit. He was becoming alive again and the fresh air filled Surge's lungs. On the third night he camped in a pub car park, high up in the hills, entered the pub and as usual chose a spot in the back between the entrance and exit.

Here he ordered mineral water and opened his book, fading into the background. A group of walkers came in demanding pints of dark beer which they drank quickly. They ordered a few more, and then a few more. Finally one of them produced a guitar and they all started to sing old folk songs. The rest of the pub joined in and as the evening went on and as the shadows grew, a feeling of bonhomie swept the pub and even Surge who was on the periphery, was caught up in the glow, quietly singing along. He went back to his tent sober, happy and contented.

Good walkers cover the 312 miles in ten days. Surge with his lope and military stride covered it in eight. On the train journey home he felt great, still too many aches and pains as he was nowhere near his old fitness but felt he was getting stronger. It had been a good test of strength but most of all endurance, being able to outlast the other man was crucial to Surge. Time to up the ante, he thought.

Back at the flat Surge changed and went shopping in a little sports shop at the top of the town buying shorts, T-shirt, socks and the most expensive, softest, most cushioned running shoes he could find. Up to now everything he had done was low impact, building up the muscles slowly and carefully, but running was a whole different ball game high impact and tough on his aging body, he was well aware that all he needed was to damage his knees or hips for the game to be over but had to take the chance time was running out. The most common problem in men of his age was shin splints when the shins got damaged due to the pounding from the pavements, good soft shoes can help but it was up to his body to cope, would it ? He started running that evening, first slowly then built up the pace. Within minutes his heart was pounding and his chest hurt but he pushed through, found the old rhythm and managed forty minutes non-stop jogging with little pain. For him at this stage he felt was a great achievement.

Over the next month running took the place of walking in his exercise regime and Surge could feel the fat dropping off him and muscle replacing it. There were still lots of aches and pains and it took an effort to resist the urge to take pain killers. He knew it was important he understood what his body was going through and how far to push, each day his strength started to return.

At the end of the second month Surge knew that he needed combat. He was stronger but rusty. It had been some time since he had really been tested in a fight. One of the biggest problems was controlling your body in a combat situation to overcome various inbuilt reactions. In action these defences want to take over, controlling adrenalin to ensure you are not swamped with the fight or flight instincts where the brain starts to shut down was one aspect; ensuring your breathing is under control was another and the main one for him was the blink reflex. Anything that looks as though it could attack the eyes causes a person to blink. If the stimulus is great you blink rapidly, this gives the brain false information. It is like looking at a flickering TV. Only a small percentage of the information gets through. The image gets blurred and both depth and distance perception is altered. The scene in front of you gets switched on and off at bewildering speeds which means you cannot judge either the attack, your response or where you are at any one point in time. Surge had always been able to control his emotions and override the blink reflex but it takes practice which only comes from action.

He found a small mixed martial arts and boxing club around a three mile run from the flat. He offered his passport with the Mark Emblem name and reference names given to him by The Grey Man plus a false address. He also paid for six months membership in advance in cash ensuring no checks were necessary. The club was new and airy. In the front was a dojo complete with mats and various training paraphernalia, mitts, sparring bags and what looked like a log with arms pointing out of it and bent wood for legs. He knew this represented a man and was used by wing chung students. Surge had spent many hours working on this piece of equipment. Surge loved the look and the smell. It was almost like home to him. How many years of his life had been spent in dojos, first being taught, then teaching. At the side of the mat were two doors which went through to the men's and women's showers and changing rooms. To the left of the mat were two sliding doors, now open that led to the boxing room with punch bags, weights, speedball and boxing ring. Here there was a smell of sweat and the curious dusty air you always get in a training room.

He quickly changed, then warmed up with skipping and then a few minutes on the heavy bag, moving from one piece of equipment to another. The dojo was empty but the boxing side had half a dozen sweaty men of all ages and sizes working away. Nobody spoke. Each went through their routines. He started now to work on upper body strength. His legs were already solid through the walking and running and his arm muscles had grown with the callisthenics but now he needed power. Surge knew that against younger, faster men he might have to take two punches against the one he could give, so when he did land a blow it had to be devastating. Surge had the knowledge of where to strike and how, built up over decades of study and practice and now worked his arms and chest to build the strength to give him the best chance, the edge.

What he really wanted though was combat. There was always someone that came to these places that wanted to dominate and bully. It took three days before he found him. The club was semi professional and their star turn was a 20 year old boxer called Steve Callan. He styled himself as 'Steve the Stinger' for his lightning jab and was a contender for the English heavyweight belt. He stood over 6ft tall and weighed an impressive 16 stone, all of which was muscle.

Surge watched him warm up. Callan ran through an impressive display of sit-ups, press ups and working the heavy bag and then went in the ring with his trainer, hitting large gloves which his trainer wore as he moved around his body. Quick, young, strong and tough, Surge watched him all evening and saw that he was also a nasty piece of work, as he started, during the sparring with the other fighters, to abuse his position, obviously leagues ahead of them. Time and again he punished anyone who joined him in the ring, taunting and cat calling any who stepped out early until the only person left was Surge working the big bag.

"Oi! Old timer," he shouted. "Fancy a few rounds?"

To the Stingers surprise, Surge nodded and stepped up into the ring. The Stinger charged in giving Surge a couple of jabs, then a left and right combination. Surge avoided one, but took the other two in face and body. The Stinger smiled. 'Lovely. No problem' he thought to himself. Over the next 15 minutes he used Surge like a punch bag, throwing punch after punch. Some got through but Surge avoided many. He moved in a really awkward strange manner, his arms sometimes flailing out towards the Stinger and then covering up so nothing could get through, his legs getting tangled inside the Stinger's. He looked like a joke but try as he did the Stinger could not land anything solid. Surge threw nothing back just absorbed the Stinger's attack. His trainer just laughed when he saw his boy was not in any trouble and let him use the time as a workout, beating on the old man.

Finally when both men were covered in sweat, he rang the bell. Surge looked grateful and got out of the ring walking unsteadily to the wall, which he lent against bending over and breathing heavily.

The Stinger shouted, "Hey Punchy! Anytime you want some more, come back." Surge just lifted his glove in salute.

However, inside Surge was elated. He could not believe how well he had done. He was playing the old dance game, manoeuvring himself into position without making the final strike, ensuring his feet hands and body were placed correctly to destroy his opponent without following through, all the time avoiding the huge punches coming his way, twisting and ducking, constantly moving under relentless, powerful pressure. One mistake and the boy would have landed a punch that could have taken Surge out but he did not make one mistake. It was like singing and swimming and playing chess at the same time, taking real concentration. He knew with absolute certainty that he could have broken this lad anytime. The boy was just meat and muscle and no brains and Surge had the measure of him.

From the moment Surge had started training he had compromised, understanding what he had been at the top of his game and now what he could be as an older man. His body was not as strong or supple as it had been and Surge had to accept it, and work out ways to compensate, calling on a life time of skill and experience. However after the bout with the boxer he now realised in combat, real violence with real pain and danger, nothing was gone. He reacted and moved as he always had. His mind, his most powerful weapon, was still attuned to being able to work on many different levels at the same time both in defence and attack. He was always two or three moves ahead of his opponent. Maybe only three or four people in the world could do that and that knowledge filled him with joy. He wanted to throw back his head and roar. He wanted to point at the Stinger and say "You are nothing!" Instead he put his head down and went to the changing room, towelled down got into his sweatpants and hoody and jogged home.

That night, alone in the dark for the first time, he felt he might be able to hold his own, might be able to finish this mission with his life and maybe some respect. All he needed was a few weeks more training and a few dozen more sessions with the Stinger.

Chapter 12

Pru stood and watched the big old man walk away to the changing room. She hated bullying and was disgusted by the way everyone had stood back and watched him get beaten up. She marched over to the trainer.

"Why did you let that happen?" she said.

"Nobody made him get in the ring," said the trainer, a balding skinny man in his fifties with BO and bad breath. "He stood up and the boy knocked him down. Should have paid for the lesson. Everyman should know his limitations."

Pru gave up, it was like talking to a brick wall , pointless, and walked away, dejected. Somehow no one ever stood up to violence. She should know. She glanced across at the full length mirror, a small woman slim women looked back at her, in her early thirties, close cropped brown hair, thin face, just plain and ordinary she thought but unbeknownst to her she was in a minority and was far more attractive than she knew. Pru had moved from Liverpool to London a year ago. Prior to that she had lived six months in a shelter. Before that hospital, victim to the beatings from her husband. They had married six years before and at first everything was great then the rows started, mainly over money. One night in a rage he had hit her. He seemed to like it and started regularly after that to lay into her for no real reason. She had no defence. Pru came from a sheltered world. Her family was upper middle class, hence the name Prudence and domestic violence was unheard of. Her dad was a gentle soul.

At first she had stayed hoping he would get better but he became worse, threatening wicked things if she ever tried to leave. Finally the beatings were so bad she was hospitalised and that's when Pru reported him to the police. A chain of events occurred. He, unbelievably ,got a suspended sentence and outside court threatened to kill her. Luckily the threat was overheard by an off duty policeman and she received a place in a woman's shelter which eventually healed her body and more importantly let her mind get stronger.

After six months she packed her bags and with help from the shelter moved to London and found a simple job in a florist shop which suited her. Pru liked the quietness and the designs, arranging the flowers in a different way each time and found for herself a more tranquil world. She rented a small flat with another woman who had a similar background and was rebuilding her life.

The gym was an idea to fight back. She had passed the sign one day on her way to work and decided on a whim that she would join, get strong and never be a victim of another man again. For the past twelve months Pru had almost lived and breathed in here. Open 24 hours a day with each member having a pass key, she came down whenever she could, built her body in the gym then enrolled in every class that would have her, from boxing to judo to jujitsu. Now she had never felt better or stronger. Her confidence growing, Pru felt she was starting to return to the real world but this time on her terms.

As the older man came out from the showers ready to leave, he passed her and Pru smelt a strange mix of sweat and soap, not at all unpleasant. She caught herself. Was she attracted to him? No, he was at least twenty years older and could have been her dad. 'Oh,' she thought, 'you do love a lost cause.' She tried to catch his eye as he walked by, to give him a smile of encouragement but he obviously did not see her.

A week went by and Pru saw the old man often. Each day he was there training with the brute Stinger beating him up regularly but the old man did not seem to mind, always raising his glove at the end as a sign of respect. Because the Stinger called him 'Punchy' that was now his nickname and everyone called him it, but most did not mean anything by it and just thought he was an ex-boxer. Many admired the way he trained outside the ring even if he was a joke inside it. He jumped rope and worked both heavy bag and speed ball with consummate ease, always in balance with plenty of power. It was just when he got into the ring, he looked so awkward falling over himself, turning into punches, not away and placing his feet all over the place, sometimes on sometimes off balance all the time the punches whipping into arms, body and face. She worried about him constantly wondering why he took these beatings.

Then something weird happened. Pru could not sleep one night and decided to go to the gym really early to burn off the insomnia. She reasoned that if her body was tired, the rest would follow. No one was in the gym and she moved through to the women's changing room. As she changed she heard movement coming from the dojo mat. Concerned that she was not alone, she wondered who might be there and stood on the bench on tip toe to look through a thin strip of glass that gave ventilation. What she saw shocked her.

The old man was stripped to the waist which was unusual for him as he always wore a loose T-shirt. His upper body was more muscular than she thought, the muscles stretched and twisted under brown skin but still strong and she could see the blue veins sticking out from his bicep muscles down to a six pack stomach. He also had on his body a number of scars, some long and jagged that looked like knife wounds and some that looked like maybe gun wounds, as she could see a puckered scar on the front that coincided with a bigger scar on the back. Could he have been a soldier, she thought. If not how did he get those scars?

What shocked her was what he was doing. First a series of stretching and tai chi moves to flex his muscles, once dropping down completely into the splits then straight up to his feet. Next a series of spins and high kicks which amazed her. Kicks that a man half his age could not have done. He then went through a beginners kata that she had learnt earlier this year but he performed it slowly and with superb skill and exquisite care, absolute perfection. Next came more advanced katas one after the other, all beautifully exercised before finishing with the most complicated set of manoeuvres she had ever seen, as close to ballet as fighting.

Initially it looked like random movement - arms, legs, elbows moving in all directions throwing kicks and punches but then he stopped and repeated the whole dance step for step. It was the most advanced kata she had ever seen. 'Where was the awkwardness now?' she thought. No question, she was watching a master at work, far in excess of her own instructors. At the end, he walked over to the block of wood with the arms sticking out and went through a series of blocks and strikes rapidly moving to a complex rhythm, not incredibly fast, but so smooth, each move slick and precise the click click click of the arms against the body filled the dojo. His muscles tensing and flowing, performing, she felt, a ritual practised countless times before.

Then Pru heard someone coming up the stairs from the outside and he stopped what he was doing, picked up his T-shirt and towel and then with his head bowed as it almost always was, he shuffled back to the boxing gym. She sat for a moment and wondered what was going on, why the play acting. He had a secret and she liked that. It was something they shared, a past not available to other people. He was really piquing her interest. She was beginning to like the old man. 'Careful Pru,' she thought. 'Careful!'

Surge knew the woman was watching him but carried on with his morning workout. He had been touched when she had talked to the Stinger's manager and part of him wanted to show her he could take care of himself and wasn't a victim but a bigger part of him just wanted to show off. He was fitter and stronger than he had been for years. His body was now moving well and as always in the gym Surge wanted to show he was better than other men. What harm could it do, he thought, and hopefully it would put her mind at rest, perhaps she would find some other lost cause to mother.

In fact the opposite happened. Surge had never been good at reading women. Pru was now fascinated and watched him out of the corner of her eye every time they were in the gym together. She noticed how he shaved every day, that his hair, even though on the surface looked unkempt, was actually trimmed neatly. She suspected he did it himself. His nails were short and spotless. Even the shapeless T-shirts and baggy sweat pants were always clean and pressed and the showers, the endless showers, he constantly showered all through the day. He would start working one part of his body then move onto the next after 40 minutes, shower and rest and then continue where he left off, constantly varying exercises, then another shower. She was convinced he was ex-military and no question, he understood yoga and tai chi though only working in the dojo when very few people were in the gym, performing gentle katas and slow movements, nothing martial at all. She never saw his full workout again.

Pru noticed how economically he worked, perfectly in balance at all times finding a rhythm in whatever he was doing, then sustaining that rhythm for an incredibly long time. He would spar with anyone who wanted to except her. She had offered a number of times and always been politely rebuffed. He always took a beating from whomever he fought, appearing incapable of fighting back. Never once did she ever see him throw a proper punch in the ring yet he was so capable. Very strange. She started to work out on equipment next to his, attempting to get him to join in a conversation but always he politely ignored her. Finally she plucked up the courage and as he was leaving walked up to him and asked, "Do you fancy going for a drink later?"

He looked at her with a strange expression on his face, then almost sadly said, "I am sorry Prudence, I have just been through a messy divorce and am not ready yet. I hope you understand."

"Sure," she said "But I was only offering a friendly drink." She raised her eyebrow as if to say he had overstepped the mark and walked away. Inside she was smiling. The divorce bit was a lie and they both knew it and best of all he had taken the time to find out her name! Just a matter of time, she thought, and she would find out his secrets, all of them.

Chapter 13

Peter Lee sat in a scruffy underground car park many miles from London with his immaculate Porsche and in his immaculate suit. Without realising it at the time, he had almost got himself in serious trouble but today with luck, would see that go away and a new chapter begin. A few months ago, since the London operation was coming along nicely, he had decided to expand into other parts of the country. He knew that rich pickings could be had in Manchester, Bradford and Leeds, home to many ethnic minorities and had started to make enquiries with some of the members of organised crime gangs in those towns.

When his mobile rang it was Stevens, the money man. Although he was from a middle class background liked to act upper class and was especially jealous of Lee's pedigree so always put on an act when he spoke to him, alluding to a common background, which is why Lee was shocked when he said, " what are you fucking trying to do? Kill us all!"

"What do you mean?" said Lee.

"Have you been digging around in Manchester,".

"Only some feelers,". "Why, what's up?"

"Listen," said Stevens. "One man controls Manchester. He is ex-spook, ex-mercenary, ex-government ex ex ex! He will fucking kill you and me if he gets wind you are starting in on his patch. What's the matter? London not rich enough for you. You are making millions."

"Calm down and tell me his name" said Lee "and if you can get me a meeting with him?".

The phone went silent and Lee could almost hear Stevens thinking.

"His name is John Sea. If you want to, I can hook you up but he does not mess around. Make no mistake if he feels you are not kosher he will make you disappear."

"Go ahead," said Lee. "Make the call. I can handle myself."

Two days later he got a call from an unknown number.

"I am from Mr Sea," a voice said with a strong Manchester accent. "I am told you would like to meet him."

"Yes," said Lee.

"Mr Sea will meet you for lunch. I will text you the details. Oh! Do not wear anything electrical. Mr Sea is very adverse to electrical items."

Which is how he found himself today in a dingy basement of a scruffy parking lot, in, of all places, Eccles, Manchester. After waiting around ten minutes, a 1960 S2 Bentley pulled up and two big men detached themselves from the front seats of the car, which was a deep dark blue and worth a small fortune. They walked half way between the two vehicles and stopped. In the dark Lee could not see their faces. He opened his door and stood with it ajar and in front of him, able to jump back in quickly if necessary.

His left hand flipped open the cleverly concealed compartment in the door card and he reached in and grabbed the gun butt. They beckoned him over.

"No. You come here," said Lee. "I want to see your faces."

The older of the two men shrugged and they both walked forward almost to the front of the Porsche.

"Mr Sea has sent me to take you to lunch."

Lee let go of the gun and flipped the lid back into place. He stepped out, closed the door and stood opposite the two men.

The younger guy walked towards him and frisked him expertly. The older man then pulled a small device from his pocket, flipped the catch and pushed the red button. There was a small woosh sound and he put the device away.

"What was that?" asked Lee.

"Mr Sea does not like electrical devices of any sort on strangers," he said. "Especially any video, cameras or recording devices. This device is based on an electromagnetic pulse and will fry any electronic chips within ten paces, hence the reason we told you not to bring any electronic devices with you and why we beckoned you to come to us.

Anything within ten paces is fucked. That will include your watch, mobile and now your car. Oh dear."

He gave a wide smile waiting for Lee to object. Lee just stood there poker faced. There was nothing on the phone of any real use in case it was stolen and as for the car it had 1960 technology so it would be fine, but clever bastards, he thought.

They walked over to the Bentley and Lee climbed in the back with the two thugs in the front, the younger one driving. Inside the car was all white leather and burr walnut and looked new. He settled back into the deep seats and looked out of the window into the grime of the back streets of Manchester and tried to relax. They drove for around forty minutes from the city deep into the countryside towards Wilmslow, until they turned into a long gravel drive. The sign advertised an exclusive golf club, spa and hotel and they drove down a meandering tarmac road until they came to what looked like an old large mansion. The car parked right outside the entrance and they walked in through the glass doors, passed a long reception desk and into the main dining room. There were a number of tables taken by the typical golfer sort all Pringle jumpers and garish colours. The room backed onto the 18th hole and the long sweeping fairway and immaculate green was visible. Everything looked expensive and he guessed the hotel was at least a five star.

To the left was a curved plate glass wall which went from floor to ceiling. The glass bottom had wheels at various intervals and was on a track to allow it to be opened and closed. Today it was closed isolating about a third of the room in which, seen through the glass, was only one table, albeit quite substantial and elegantly set against the far window with a large empty carpeted space between it and the glass and the main dining area. At the table sat an average sized man in green checked golfing trousers and Pringle jumper, standard golfing wear. He lounged in the chair, one leg over the arm. Lee was taken over and a door opened in the glass wall. The dining room was noisy with customers but once Lee was inside and the door closed, 90% of the noise disappeared, adding to the air of privacy and ownership. Lee was now in this man's domain. As he walked to the table the man stood up and walked towards him unsmiling. He stretched out his hand and they shook.

"Sit down" said John Sea.

Lee appraised the person in front of him. He was late forties with brown, close cropped hair and a handsome, yet strong face. It reminded Lee of a boxer he had once known. The man looked fit, tough and radiated authority.

A waiter walked over and Lee ordered mineral water and Sea ordered a scotch and soda. Once the waiter had left, Sea leaned forward and speaking in a quiet but strong Mancunian accent said, "I have been told that you have tried to muscle in on my territory. Is that right"?

"Yes" said Lee "Until I found out it was your territory, then I stopped."

"Very wise" said Sea "For I would have chopped your bollocks off if you hadn't."

Sea spoke the threat with no menace, change of pitch or facial expression. It was more frightening because of that. Lee knew he was dealing with a hard man. "What's your pitch?" said Sea.

Over the next 40 minutes Lee went through the set up, explaining in detail where the drugs came from, how they were sent, picked up, cut and distributed. He laid out the financial costs and return, only going into detail when Sea asked for specific clarification but keeping the relevant names and places from him so as to ensure he could not cut him out. Lee had prepared well and laid out the plan like a military operation with detailed pricing, statistics and risk evaluations. At the end of it there was a silence as Sea lent back in his chair to think. Lee knew this was the time to go silent, not overcook the presentation.

Finally Sea lent forward and looked Lee in the eye. "You are at a crossroads," he said. "And I will give you two directions to take, both life changing. The first one is that you get up and walk away, never setting foot on my patch again. The second is that I get my people to check your story. If it proves that you are snowing me you will get a visit and be chopped into tiny pieces, slowly. If you are genuine we may have a deal. What do you want to do?"

"I want to go for it," said Lee.

"OK," said Sea. "My guys will take you back to your car. Expect a call one way or the other next week."

They shook hands and Lee walked out, beads of sweat drying on his brow.

Chapter 14

The Grey Man was finally finished. He had found out most of the information he needed and now knew of the various organisations involved and enough of the day-to-day working to flush out the top men. Despite himself he was impressed with the simplicity and ingenuity of the scheme. Time to bring this to a close, he thought and made a call to The Firm, they gave him an address of an old private school in Horsham and he spent the afternoon driving down. When he arrived waiting for him was a kindly looking old man who introduced himself as the headmaster. The Grey Man felt he had met him many years before, sure that he had once been in the business. The Grey Man explained what he needed and was shown to the old gatehouse building, now faded and with the windows partially boarded, it had obviously been empty for some time. They went through the heavy oak door and up the stairs into a small room with an entrance and fire escape exit. The Grey Man approved. He always like two ways out.

"Can you ensure everyone is kept away?" he asked.

"Of course," said the headmaster. "Should be easy as no one is allowed near the building since it was condemned."

"Thank you," said The Grey Man. "We will be finished here on Tuesday at 14.00."

The headmaster dismissed, wandered away and The Grey Man walked back to where he had parked the car. It was a new black Mercedes with dark tinted windows. From the boot he picked up a number of boxes and carried them back into the gatehouse up to the room and opened them, removing some items, then back downstairs before walking a circle around the building dropping small devices every ten yards or so onto the path and covering them with dust and gravel. He locked the car and then went inside closing and locking the front door of the gatehouse and started work, first hanging heavy black drapes over every window, then activating the sensors he had dropped, feeding these back to his computer. He also installed a number of motion sensors in the hall and on the landing plus under all the windows.

Next he hacked into the school CCTV system and overrode the camera looking at the gate house. That feed would only come to his computer. The school monitoring system would just see a black image and could not record any comings and goings. He also hacked into the digital recording section and erased his meeting with the headmaster from the security systems hard disk. Then set up the white noise systems which would stop anyone from eavesdropping. This essentially scrambled any voice frequencies making them intelligible to anyone on the outside of the room using remote listening devices. Finally he set up the projector and screen. Once this was done The Grey Man sent out the message to Collins, Surge and the boy Jon. Once all was complete, he set out his camp bed, lay back and looked around the dingy, cobweb ridden room. How many had he slept in? 'Too many,' he thought.

His mind ran to the two men he was involved with. Their lives had intertwined many times over the years and in a moment of sadness realised that in a life time of loneliness they were his only friends. He thought back to the first time he had heard of the man they now called Surge. A rumour had gone around that he was special when he first joined the force but it was his passing out that started the legend and forced The Grey Man at that time to pull his file.

The Grey Man had a fantastic memory and lying on his camp bed could remember the file almost word for word. From borstal Surge had gone through an induction course and then a series of standard self defence classes finding himself, in many cases, far in advance of the training program. As his instructors got better and the training more advanced, he got stronger and his fitness became legendary as was his solitary behaviour, always very self contained, he appeared to prefer his own company whenever possible. Gradually though as he started to feel part of the military family Surge started to thaw and became an integral part of any unit he joined whilst never talkative, he found ways to bond with other soldiers, following the same interests as himself. Surge quickly specialised in unarmed combat and went beyond normal training seeking out doctors, both surgeons and neurologists to work out the bodies weaknesses, learning how and where to strike for maximum effectiveness, becoming very quickly something of an expert at a very young age.

Within two years of joining he could beat anyone they sent against him so sometimes in mock field operations, they set him against two or more men. This got dangerous as Surge had no compunctions about breaking and wounding an opponent. Winning was all he wanted. Whilst most man would stop before he injured another, Surge would follow through, and in the end as his reputation grew, they stopped any training with hand to hand combat.

In the third year they sent him on a course to a special military training school in Japan which specialised in unarmed combat especially the one strike attack. It was recognised as the best in the world. He was the only white man that had ever been given the opportunity to attend and at first the Japanese instructors resented this young westerner. By the end of the nine months, he had absorbed all their knowledge and was taking the training into new areas of technique and research, all deadly, at the end they begged him to stay but he was not even slightly tempted. He wanted the real thing, to be in operations. So Surge came back.

In England and now at the end of his training they set him on the normal finishing course for a Special Operations Operative, called a rabbit hunt. The idea was both to show him how far he had come but also his limitations and add a little humility. They first filled his Bergan rucksack with 80lbs of house bricks and gave him a standard issue rifle and water bottle to carry. He was told he had 24 hours to complete a fifty mile march across country using map and compass. Once Surge had completed this and when he thought they were heading back to barracks, he was picked up by helicopter and flown to the Brecon Beacons, a wild rough part of Wales used by the SAS and Commandos for endurance training. Stripped of everything but his uniform, he was told to stand to attention in the freezing cold wind.

"You have 10 hours to reach a RDZ 30 miles away," said the smiling sergeant. "But in 30 minutes a pack will start to chase you down. Some of the hardest bastards I know and when they catch you, will give you the kicking of your fucking lifetime, you smug bastard. Now run!"

It was a classic rabbit chase. He was already tired and now they would let him run and when totally exhausted, would pick him up and take him to an interrogation centre for a further three days of sleep deprivation and questioning. This would break him and show him he was no superman. Every man must know his limitations, was there current doctrine.

The team selected were all SAS as the brass knew he was special. They were fit and strong and experienced, but as the helicopter landed they were called forward and given an extra briefing.

"Watch this one. He is a tough bastard, run him hard and only tackle him when he is exhausted."

"No problem," the experienced team leader shouted back over the helicopter rotors. They had all played the game before and were looking forward to it.

Each of the SAS Team were found over the next fifteen hours in various places all along the route, all trussed up with their own webbing. Each soldier had one broken bone, finger, rib, collar bone, or ankle and the officers in charge found Surge at the RDZ asleep under a bush looking none the worse for the outing. When he was asked why the broken bones, he said, "I don't like being a rabbit."

The Grey Man loved him for that. His operational career and legend started that day.

The Grey Mans mind turned to Collins, who he was convinced, was a borderline schizophrenic. On one side, the family man, the gentle soul that warmed him to so many, on the other side, the cold blooded killer who could pull a trigger and end a man's life without blinking or it affecting him in any way. He was not the fastest. The Grey Man had seen quicker men on the draw but he was by far the best shot with the most confidence. As he pointed the gun he hit the target, no thought at all that he might miss, quite uncanny.

There was one job he had been on with Collins that stood out in The Grey Man's mind over so many. A gun dealer in the Ukraine playing both sides in a very messy game. A directive came down from on high that he was to be killed publicly and clinically, no bombs or long range rifles. A message was to be sent. If you cross us, we can get you anywhere, anytime, easily. Unfortunately it was anything but easy. The gun dealer had two exceptional bodyguards, ex-KGB who were amongst the best available, able and willing to shield the mark and return fire with lethal uzi sub-machine guns which they carried at all times in shoulder holsters. The Grey Man knew that to get to the mark these men would also have to be taken out or the world would explode around anyone near.

The Grey Man had worked through all scenarios but because there were three to target simultaneously, it meant at least two shooters. It was bad enough getting one in tight without being spotted but how to get two men close who could work in perfect coordination was next to impossible against such experienced guards.

Eventually he asked Collins for his opinion.

"No worries," said The Assassin. "I can do it on my own. Just get me close."

Having no other options The Grey Man said, "OK. Your funeral."

The day of the hit The Grey Man was in a second floor apartment two miles from the hotel that housed the gun dealer. The Assassin was outside the hotel leaning against the wall around the corner from the front lobby. The Grey Man had hacked into the hotel CCTV both in the lobby and outside and could monitor both on a single screen. He saw the mark leave the elevator, one body guard in front, one closely behind. They moved fast. The Grey Man alerted Collins and he started to walk forward, timing his stride carefully, not too fast not too slow, unbuttoning his over coat but leaving the top button still connected so the coat gaped like a cape as he walked. The Grey Man saw the coming together just as the limousine drew up with the doors opening, two guns magically appeared in The Assassin's hands and before the guards could reach halfway to their weapons, two shots rang out one after the other but amazingly all three men dropped. The Assassin sheathed his guns, turned the corner and disappeared.

The Grey Man went over and over the hit. There had definitely only been two shots fired but three bodies. That night he asked Collins how he had killed three men with two bullets.

"Not two, but four bullets," said The Assassin.

"But I only heard two shots" said The Grey Man.

The Assassin smiled, "I drew both guns and triggered them together. The left hand shot the right bodyguard, the right hand shot the mark in the head and then I moved my left hand to shoot the other bodyguard. With my right hand I shot the mark in the heart, double tap. Both guns triggered twice, four shots in all. Both guns were fired simultaneously, hence you only heard two shots."

He made it sound easy like rubbing your stomach and patting your head at the same time.

The following day The Grey Man, no stranger to guns spent hours in the shooting range trying to duplicate the feat. It was, he decided, impossible.

He thought how long ago both these incidents had been. Collins was nearly the same age as The Grey Man and he knew how much that would slow him down, as he lay there his back, his joints, all ached and both his hearing and his eyesight were not as good as they had once been. For an assassin, body and eye control were everything. And what about Surge? He had been genuinely shocked when he had seen him looking old and fat. In a profession like his when most are over the hill at thirty five, Surge had lasted ten more years because of his exceptional skill and fitness. Now in his fifties, what will he do against anyone younger with just a modicum of skill? That's of course, not even factoring in what happened in Ireland.

The Grey Man remembered that sadness like it was yesterday. Surge, who had been at the top of the tree for nearly twenty five years, was sent to Northern Ireland for what should have been a simple dead letter drop. He could have passed it to a junior but was bored and looking for a bit of excitement. He was over confident. There had been little trouble there for some time and he expected an easy trip. Because of this his radar was down he, unbelievably for Surge, walked into a dark room with no exits. A trip wire pulled his legs from under him and five men set about him with baseball bats. He still managed to break one before passing out, but even though unconscious they continued to beat him until most of the bones in his body were cracked or broken. A weaker man would have died. As it was he spent nine months in hospital, many in traction, with the doctors marvelling at his recovery.

This is when Collins had approached him and offered the deal. Finally Surge discharged himself and everyone thought he would be hell bent on revenge. The Grey Man had even found out their names and where they lived but more than Surge's body had been broken, his spirit appeared to have gone as well. Refusing to even think about vengeance, he retired and cut himself off from everyone and started to drink.

For the first time Surge had found his limitations and it had finished him. What would he be like now, thought The Grey Man? Would he be able to step up and take on these men face to face? The Grey Man's plan was dependant on Surge being able to handle some of the soldiers and flush out the top men. What if he had become an embarrassment and is beaten? They had no backup and the men they were hunting were young vicious violent men.

Chapter 15

The call went out. Jon had been waiting now for weeks and was sitting in a lecture when he heard the beep of an incoming text. He looked down and saw an address and a time. His heartbeat soared and excusing himself from the class sidled sideways down the row of chairs. The lecturer even though his class was disturbed, ignored him and kept on talking. Jon rushed to his room, threw some clothes into a bag and ran to the Audi. Once inside he placed the key in the ignition and before turning the key stopped and just sat there looking out of the windscreen as a wave of despair hit him and a cold fear descended. He had everything, good education, prospects, friends, money ,everything a boy of his age could want and now he was rushing headlong into some serious shit. He had never had so much as a parking ticket, certainly not got into any real trouble. In fact could not remember ever even getting into a fight. Now he was talking violence and murder, and would face perhaps his own death or see his fathers. Failing that, a life in prison. It all seemed so unbelievable, how could three old men and him take on organised crime and get away with it? It did not make any sense. Don Quixote tipping at the windmill came to mind. He felt like calling his dad and backing out but knew he would not. How could he leave his father at this time? Jon let his anger overtake his fear. The bastards had killed his mother and his father was walking into danger. Time to become a man, he thought and damn the consequences. Whatever happened he knew his life would never be the same again. Jon started the engine, took one last look over his shoulder at the university, a life he had longed for, had worked hard for and would probably never return to, and gunned the car from the parking space.

Collins was in the shop when the text arrived. He finished serving, told Eli to go home early and that he would be in touch and waited for the customer to leave. He then turned the sign on the door to closed and reached for his coat, turned off all the lights, locking the shop as he went. His mind was calm and as he stepped out on his final operational journey he had made a decision. Follow The Grey Man, kill those men, then come back, sell the shop and take Jon with him home to Israel.

Surge was in the gym which is almost where he lived now when the text came through. He showered, dressed and walked down the street, his mind in turmoil. He felt physically stronger and fitter, though still old. His body moved as well as he could make it but it ached and his stamina which used to be legendary was now suspect, as was his knee and back. Would it be enough against stronger, younger fitter men? Time to find out, he thought. It was easy being brave when you were up against weaker men. Could he still be as brave now? Surge took a deep breath filling his lungs then smiled a grim smile. He had been a hard man all his life and deep down knew he still was. He had heart, skill and a lifetime of knowledge. It would be enough. It had to be. He had promised Collins, given his word. For that is all he had left, his word. Courage he had left in Ireland, dignity he lost in the hospital as a broken man crying in Collins arms. He would do this last thing whatever it cost and only death would stop him fulfilling his promise.

The Grey Man had everything set up in the corner. A projector balanced on an old desk connected to a laptop. He had chairs set up in a semi-circle across from a pull down screen. Jon and Collins arrived first and as they waited, each man wondered what the three months had done to Surge. How much can you pull back in such a short time? Collins had decided that friend or no friend, if Surge had not changed he would scrub him from the operation and find another way.

Finally they heard him coming up the stairs and as they saw him jaws dropped and smiles broke out. He was dressed in a smart pair of jeans with brown loafers and a polo shirt. He had shaved his head and looked sharp. His waist was at least four inches smaller, his chest and arms bigger, the fat had drained from his face and neck. He looked ten years younger - fit and strong. Finally Jon saw the man his father had described. There was something hard about him that made you look at your own manliness. Made you wonder if you could you measure up to him. Definitely an alpha male.

"Well done," said Collins taking Surge's hand. "You look great. How do you feel?"

"Ready," replied Surge and smiled back.

They sat in their chairs and The Grey Man turned the lights down. The windows were blacked out with the drapes and there was a faint hum in the air, not enough to intrude but constantly there and Jon noticed a smell of ozone as the white boxes did their trick. The Grey Man brought a number of cameras onto the screen that were surrounding the building they were in and checked some software on the scanners. "We are alone, it seems," and in his best Jackanory voice said, "If everyone is comfortable, I will begin."

"The operation is impressive. As Collins has previously explained it is about sending drugs into this country to ethnic people who already have legitimate contacts abroad and bring in various legitimate products. The drugs are just slipped in with the rest. Some are willing recipients and are paid. Some are reluctant and have been forced. Because of their background they are all reluctant to involve the police. Targets are mainly Pakistani, Bangladeshis, Afghans and Indians. The reason you as a Jew were targeted is because of your import business, not the shop."

Collins nodded and The Grey Man continued. "Even if caught with the parcels, the penalties are not high and the distinction in UK law between cut and uncut heroin does not exist, so a few grams of uncut heroin, which could be cut into a kilo of junk, is just treated as a few grams of heroin. Arguments are being made to the police by the few receivers that have been arrested that they are innocent victims and it is all a big mistake, for a first offence they each received a slapped wrist. Actually so far this operation boasts that no one who has been caught has been prosecuted. Small and often slips through the net. The Customs officers are looking for that big score."

"The whole pick up operation in London is outsourced to local villains, bought with a sweet deal offering the current drug dealers half the price they had been paying from other sources plus a purer drug which can be further cut."

"These local villains were all running some kind of protection racket as well as pushing drugs and as the need for more delivery addresses grew, so the operation branched in that direction, involving victims already paying protection as long as they fitted the demographic."

"The man who visited you in the shop," he said to Collins. "Is undoubtedly inner circle and likes to set the deals up using the locals just as couriers. So drugs are harvested along the Pakistani and Afghan borders, broken down into small packages and then shipped to these UK addresses. These arrive alongside the legitimate packages that the person had ordered. In effect it blends in and is difficult to spot. It is then picked up from the receivers by the locals, taken to a centre and cut and distributed. Simple and easy."

"London is broken into four geographical areas each one with its own mob. They hate each other but know better than to get into war. Each gang pays the operation the same price for the drugs and uses the same mark up, keeping the street price constant across London. Each making the same profit depending on the amount of receivers. Payment is convoluted but ends up with a man called Stevens who apparently launders the money."

"Stevens is well known and protected, phenomenally rich and well connected. I have come across him before when dealing with The Firm, we need to be careful dealing with him. Business is so good that they have flooded London with heroin and are now starting to export into other regions of the UK and Europe. Literally hundreds of people are involved and the quantities are staggering. The receivers involved however do not know each other and work independently. It is only at the top that the organisation comes together. No one in the customs department would believe that this could have been set up and managed with so many different people involved but it is not only working, it is thriving."

"How do we break it up?" said Collins. "Through this man Stevens? He must know who the top men are."

"Stevens is not the way," replied The Grey Man. "He is too well protected and he has fingers in too many pies. Who knows what or who could come out of the woodwork? Tracking down the ringleaders of this operation would be very difficult in amongst all his other scams. There is a much simpler way to flush them out. The gangs as I have said hate each other and constantly needle. Any sign of weakness from any one of them and they would be pounced upon by the others. They all live in constant fear of each other. I suggest this. We hit three of their pickups in three different gang areas, leaving the fourth to take the blame. Very quickly war would start and everything would grind to a halt. This should bring in the organisation's top men to quieten things down and see what is happening. Once they expose themselves, I can isolate and track them down."

"The secret is to hit all three quickly, one straight after another to give the illusion that this is one of the gang's muscling in. As you can imagine, these guys do not work to a timetable but I have a list of the latest parcels, coming in and where they will be picked up from. The gangs tend to set their member's areas so I know who should pick them up. Obviously no one wants the parcel at the receiver for very long so drop off and pick up is agreed in advance and I have managed to isolate a few for us to hit and if we move quickly we can knock one down after another."

He turned to Jon. "Can you ride a motorbike?"

"Sure," said Jon. "I passed my test last year."

"Good," said The Grey Man.

He turned to Surge. "This all depends on you. Two hits are simple, the third could be very difficult."

"What do you have?" said Surge.

"This is the first guy," said The Grey May hitting a button on his laptop. A video was projected onto the screen. A heavy set balding man appeared in a brown overcoat.

"Mark number one, Tony Morris," said The Grey Man. "He is forty two years old, part bouncer, part runner, a bit of a gopher. He has had two stretches inside, one for eighteen months, one for two years, both for grievous bodily harm fighting in nightclubs. Drinks too much and likes to work alone."

"Any martial arts training or boxing?" asked Surge.

"Nothing as far as I can see," continued The Grey Man. "Just a big no talent thug. He is also not that observant, without even the basic surveillance checks. He is like a milk man on his round, mostly bored."

"This is the place that will have the first parcel," he said showing video of the thug walking into a Bangladeshi restaurant and within thirty seconds was back on the pavement stuffing a package into his pocket. "Not very subtle," The Grey Man said smiling. Next he displayed a plan of the restaurant and the street it was on and showed Surge where he could stand and be unobserved.

"Try to take him from behind," he said. "The less you can be described the better."

He then zoomed out to the surrounding area and explained to Jon where to park the motorbike.

"Do not have the engine running. That just attracts attention. Look ordinary but study your mirrors. As Surge comes towards you, I want the engine started, into first gear, foot on the brake before Surge gets to you. Then pull away sharply, but not fast. Do not squeal the tyres. From then on follow Surge's instructions, he will know if you are being followed. I will also be watching you remotely. From there you drive to here," and he punched up a map and picture on the screen. "Drive this route to mark number two." He showed another map and picture. "You will have seven minutes, tops."

Another man's face appeared on the screen, much younger, early twenties, clean shaven, T-shirt and jeans.

"This one," said The Grey Man. "Is Phil Murphy and he is on his way up, a real wheeler dealer. Sees these pickups as no brainers and takes no precautions at all. More of a street punk, in and out of borstal, more mouth than muscle. But beware Surge, he is street smart, fast and always carries a knife which he likes to use. OK so far?"

"Sure" said Surge.

"Right," said The Grey Man continuing. "This is the shop." The video rolled. It was a corner newsagent with baskets and fruit piled up outside. In a row of shops like thousands of other such shops in London. The younger man was in and out quickly, the shop keeper obviously waiting for him. He was then seen jogging down to a small hatch back Honda. He looked neither right nor left.

"He always tries to park in the same spot. It has plenty of cover. I would suggest that you wait by his car."

Surge nodded.

"Again try to hit him from behind if possible."

"Jon, you pick Surge up from here," he said pointing out a spot on the map. "And as fast as you are able bring him to the tube station here." Another image flashed on the screen. "There will be a change of clothes in the top box. Take Surge's crash helmet and put it into the empty top box, drive to here, around five miles away, lock the bike and helmets as you found them and drop the keys down a drain when you are well away from the bike. Then travel by bus to the rendezvous spot. I will give you the address."

He turned his attention back to Surge.

"Now once Jon drops you off, catch the Northern and then Central line to this spot. Collins will meet you there and drive to this place two miles away. The whole journey needs to take no longer then 20 minutes." He paused and looked around the room. "This is when it gets tricky," he said and he pulled up on the computer screen two men's faces, one mid thirties, ordinary looking, close cropped hair, tattooed arms and neck. The other man was about the same age but big and heavily muscled with a flat hard face that looked as if it had had its fair share of beatings.

"These two work as a pair," The Grey Man said. "The smaller man, Mickey Jones is the driver, big mouth but no trouble. The big one however is a different kettle of fish. He is the muscle and is very, very dangerous. He specialises in mixed martial arts, cage fighting. Surge, very nasty. He holds a black belt in karate and aikido and loves the violence. They call him Billy the Bull. Two stints inside prison, twelve months and two years both for beating men to a pulp. You need to be very careful with this one and blind side him. If you go head to head the deal's blown. He will rip you apart. He is not going to go down quickly or quietly. The added difficulty is that you need to take him and the smaller man out at the same time as Mickey watches the Bull's back from inside the car. He is very alert, constantly working the road, very sharp."

"The only way I can work it out," he continued flashing another picture onto the screen. "Is if you stand in this alley opposite the restaurant which is the pickup spot. Mickey normally parks here as it gives him the very best view of the street. The alley is behind him to the right. You should be able to fit into his blind spot on his mirror. How you get to him is up to you as he will be inside the car and you will have to be very quick. Once you have taken him out you can see from this angle that just in front of the corner shop is a telephone box, which you can use to block yourself from the Bull as he walks back to the car. If lucky, you break him from behind, not perfect but achievable. However I think you need to see this."

He ran a short video of the Bull's last cage fight win. It was vicious, short and bloody. Surge studied the way the Bull moved, looking intently at the screen then asked to have it run again.

"I wish I could have found you an easier third target," said The Grey Man. "But timing is everything and he always visits this shop at the same time like clockwork on his way to the gym and I can guarantee if they keep to the normal routine, they will be there. Three hits in 30 minutes. No one will suspect that one man could have carried it off."

"Are you sure we need to do this?" said Collins. "Would two hits not be enough? This looks far too dangerous."

The Grey Man shook his head, "I don't think so. I feel a minimum of three hits leaving one gang untouched. That's where everyone will point the finger. It needs to be done like this for maximum disruption and to demonstrate a serious threat to the organisation."

They all looked to Surge.

"What do you think?" said Collins "This big guy is no fool and you need to hit both quickly."

"No sweat," replied Surge.

Collins lent across looking Surge deep in the eyes. "Do not fight this guy," he said. "If it goes wrong, Surge, hit the deck and I will blow him away. OK?"

"Sure," said Surge. "When do we go?"

"Today's Monday. This all goes off Wednesday," said The Grey Man. "Any questions?" They all shook their heads and The Grey Man went through the plan another three times. Each time they added a detail or two. The route was imprinted into Jon's head and The Grey Man explained,

"You must drive only this way. There are thousands of CCTV cameras in London on this route which I can use to see you and ensure you are not followed. I can also block or override them so you will disappear from the system permanently. Do you understand? When this hits the fan the whole of London's underground will be hunting you. We must leave no clue."

"Once this is finished, Surge back to the gym, Collins to the shop, Jon home. Thursday morning, Jon you pick up Surge and meet me and your father back here. We will lay low and see where the game takes us. I will have everything hooked into the phones of these guys. As soon as we identify the top players we move. This could all be over Thursday night."

Jon took Surge back to his flat. They hardly spoke, both deep in their thoughts. He dropped him 100 yards from the door and as he opened the door Surge leaned across and for the first time shook Jon's hand.

"Don't worry kid," he said. "We have done this all before. Watch my lead and follow instructions to the letter, OK."

"OK," said Jon and then Surge was gone.

Surge watched the car drive away. He had mixed emotions. The boy was so new to all this but he has good genes he thought. He will do. He went in and headed for the bedroom. In the closet were all the clothes he had bought from the charity shops he had visited on that Sunday afternoon. He set about laying out the changes. It was essential, even though he would, as much as possible, avoid getting seen, that if he was he could not be recognised. There was always the worry of a random passer-by with a sharp eye. Surge knew the trick to any disguise was to make one bold statement, be a stereotype. Any untrained eye would fill in the details even if they were not there. So, if in a mechanics overall they would supply the grease even if he was clean faced. If he dressed older they would see the lines, if younger, the spring in his step. Be a type, not an individual he could hear his trainer saying.

Surge knew that getting Mickey and the Bull would be hard. He did not want to take on both of them at the same time and could not have Mickey warning the Bull either. Mickey had to go out very quick and clean. He needed a bit of help, an edge, so wandered down to the hardware shop and bought a fine engineer's file, then onto an old army surplus store that sold all kinds of weapons from combat knives and swords to martial arts weapons. The old boy who ran it had a smile for Surge, perhaps recognising that he was ex-army. Through the counter glass Surge spotted what he wanted. It was a bar of steel approximately five inches long with a domed point at one end and a key ring at the other. It looked like the kind of key ring you had on a holiday home, big and clumsy and difficult to lose. He bought it and wandered home. In the kitchen he placed a sheet of newspaper on the table and started to file the bar making the domed end more tapered. It looked innocuous but Surge had trained with this weapon in Japan. Called a koboken it was designed to be held in the fist with an inch protruding from the bottom and then to be slammed down on head, shoulders and joints. The tapered end focused the blow. Heavy steel plus technique could easily break any bone in the body. A lethal weapon but if Surge was stopped by the police it would just look like a hefty key ring and fob.

Once he had the end filed to his satisfaction, Surge clutched it in his fist and slammed down hard. The koboken tip smashed right through the wooden table leaving a round hole , perfect. He now just had to manoeuvre himself into a position to use it. He put the koboken with the clothes, changed and jogged to the gym.

As always Pru was waiting and over the last few weeks it had become easier for him to acknowledge her than ignore her. He told himself that any man with a pretty woman chasing him who ignored her would stand out. That was the last thing he wanted.

So Surge had started to help her in her training, holding the heavy bag and spotting for her on the weights. She talked incessantly and he normally smiled and let it flow. In truth he enjoyed training with her and the touch of humanity it bought to his life. Lonely by nature, she bought home what he had been missing in his life. There had been women but truth to tell, not many. In the early days Surge had enjoyed the life of the warrior monk. Once in the army he had kept away from the brothels and whores frequented by many. Later in Special Services and working for The Firm, there had been a few female operatives but the nature of their business did not allow for long term relationships. It was hard enough keeping yourself alive without worrying about others and a family at home can leave you vulnerable, hence the current operation. He did not want or need any complications. He decided that once all this was over he would disappear leaving Pru none the wiser.

Pru knew she was getting through to Mark Emblem. Each day the ice melted just a little more. Twice now they had gone for coffee after training and each time was longer then the last. He was an interesting talker on many subjects as long as you did not ask him any questions about his past and unusually was also a good listener. Once a Russian couple came in the coffee shop looking for directions, speaking in broken English and Mark had answered them in what sounded like fluent Russian much to the couple's amazement. She wondered what was stopping him from taking the next step with her. In looks he had improved from the sad old man a few months ago to a strong, powerful middle aged man that moved beautifully. His face was now chiselled with deep brown eyes and when he smiled, which she admitted was rare, his face lit up and made him handsome. The only thing spoiling their time together was the sparring with the Stinger as the bouts were getting nastier and nastier. The Stinger knew he could not get hurt as Mark hardly ever hit back so the Stinger just unloaded with every punch he had in his repertory. Most ended up getting blocked on arms and elbows but too many got through. Mark just went through his strange bobbing and weaving moves with his legs everywhere and arms flailing. She could see no sense in it and one day pleaded with him not to spar. He just looked at her and said "It's a gym. Why do you think I am here?"

"I have no idea," she said "Why are you here?"

A frosty silence descended. She knew he had a secret and that she had come a bit too close. Mark turned away and just got on with his training.

At the end of that Monday session just as she was leaving he came to her.

"Look," he said. "In a few days I have to go away for work. I could be some time, OK."

"Sure," she said puzzled.

"I just thought you should know I am not leaving because of you or because I did not want to know you better. It's just business."

"How long will you be gone?" she asked.

"Maybe a couple of years if the contract goes well," he replied.

"Oh," she said, smiled, nodded her head and walked down the street.

He could see before she turned away the tears forming and he felt bad. Surge knew that he should not have told her but did not want any investigation into his disappearance. He had to ensure no one would come looking for Mr Emblem. This operation was closing and it was nearly time, if he survived, to move on. As she walked away a terrible wave of loneliness and regret hit him far harder than he expected. Surge tried to shrug it off but it stayed with him for the rest of the day. He went home and slept fitfully.

Chapter 16

On the morning of the operation Surge rose early and went for a run, just as he normally did, came back and showered and changed. Jon picked him up in the Audi at the designated spot. Surge had everything he needed in a small black sports bag.

They drove to the first position and Surge quietly went through the plan again with Jon.

"Remember do nothing that will attract attention. No gunning engines or rubber necking to see where I am. While you are waiting, take out your newspaper or pretend to check the bike. Become invisible by being normal. Is that clear?"

"Sure," said Jon.

"Another thing and I mean this," said Surge. "If you see me in trouble, drive off. Do not come and try to help. I will be able to find a way out but cannot be looking after you as well. Finally after all this, be alert without being obvious. Use your peripheral vision to search for anyone or anything that should not be there. If you feel something is wrong, drive away. Remember I will cope. The last thing I need Jon is to walk back into a trap because you have not paid attention. Is that clear?"

"Sure, sure," said Jon. "I won't let you down."

Surge smiled. "You have good blood, kid," he said kindly. "I know you will be true."

Jon could almost feel the buzz, the energy coming from the big man. This is what he did, what he was made for. They shook hands solemnly.

"See you on the other side," Surge said and climbed out of the car.

Jon immediately drove off and went to the allotted dropping place. He parked the car, took the black sports bag from the rear seats, put the keys in the glove box, stepped out and while walking away, dialled a number which locked the car doors.

To the left was a small alley way. He walked two hundred yards down it and turned left. Parked there was a big Honda 650cc trials bike complete with a helmet attached to the frame by a lock and a top box. He went over and unlocked the top box, took out the second helmet and put it on, putting the sports bag into the top box. He unlocked the helmet on the frame but left it fastened. He started up the engine and drove to the RDZ a mile away.

Surge was now dressed in a dirty mechanics boiler suit complete with an oily baseball hat. He checked his watch, 8.30am and walked towards the shop.

Tony Morris appeared. Big, scruffy and unshaven wearing the same brown overcoat as on the screen at the briefing. He looked neither right nor left just walked directly through the doors of the restaurant. Surge pretended to window shop in a row of shops opposite but kept his eye on him as he talked to the owner, who then passed him a small parcel which he pocketed and turned to leave. Morris walked out the restaurant and marched down the road without a care in the world.

Surge timed his approach carefully. Morris walked directly towards Surge passing him on the right, oblivious to his presence. As they came close, Surge put his right hand in the boiler suit pocket and made a fist, with his thumb on top of the fist rather than wrapped around the fingers, he pushed the joint of the thumb up making a point. He moved forward slowly and casually, just a man out shopping, having gauged the distance between them looked away.

As they drew level Surge's arm snapped out just in front of Morris's chest and then sharply up, his hand almost touching his coat running up close to his neck, the joint of Surge's thumb striking in between and just behind Morris's chin directly into the nerve. This nerve is protected by the chin bone and when caught just right from behind it causes an instant knockout. A full punch on the chin causes the chin to push back into this nerve and also produces the same result. The classic boxers knockout. The move was done so quickly that no one noticed, least of all Morris who collapsed unconscious hitting the ground hard. Surge lent over, reached inside his pocket, picked up the package and was around the corner in a split second, just as passers-by were coming to the man's aid. He knew that Morris would be out for three to five minutes and when he woke would have no recollection at all of what had happened. There would be no pain in his chin, just pain from the fall. Perfect.

As Surge moved he stripped off the overalls and baseball cap, rolled them into a ball and without stopping pushed them into a public bin. He was now dressed in a blue sweat shirt with jeans. At the second corner, just back from the road was Jon on the bike. He threw the spare helmet at Surge and started the engine. Surge opened the top box and put the parcel inside, he then jumped on behind Jon and they drove off winding through the traffic. Jon drove fast and accurately in and out of the crowded roads covering an impressive amount of distance in a short time without bringing any undue attention. Once they arrived at the next stop Surge got off, handed the helmet to Jon and pulled a battered three quarter length leather jacket from the sports bag in the top box, another charity shop purchase. He put it on as he walked away pulling up the collar. From the side pocket he took out a pair of aviator style sunglasses which obscured his eyes and with his chin down, collar up, he effectively masked most of his face. As he neared the shopping centre he slowed down. Nothing there. Either Phil Murphy was late or maybe Surge was early. He sauntered along slowly before with some relief saw Murphy drive up and park, wheels screeching in a noisy bright canary yellow customised Peugeot 205, probably the most garish car in the street and a ridiculous choice for conducting illegal activities.

'Amateurs,' Surge thought. 'How over confident this team must be!' He reached into the other pocket of the coat and pulled out a newspaper and lent against the fence by the Peugeot, opening the newspaper to further hide his face as Murphy got out and disappeared inside the restaurant. Thirty seconds later he was out jogging to the car, bleeping the door locks. As he reached for the handle, Murphy turned his back and Surge moved, stepping forward and rabbit punching him behind the ear, a short powerful jab. Murphy's face slammed into the glass. As he slipped down the door Surge retrieved the package and was away before Murphy hit the ground. Walking fast and purposefully he turned down a narrow alley. The jacket and sunglasses were thrown over a fence along with the sweat shirt. Now he had on a white polo shirt and jeans. Almost too easy, Surge thought. They had no skills, no class.

At the bike he could see how white Jon's face was. 'Sometimes,' thought Surge. 'It is harder to wait than be in the thick of the action.' He threw on the helmet and jumped on quickly as Jon shot away flying down the road far above the speed limit. Surge shouted for him to slow down. Jon's nerves were ragged but he complied, concentrating on following The Grey Man's route. At the tube station, Surge put the package and the helmet into the top box and took out a blue jumper and another baseball hat from the bag which he put on. He looked at Jon.

"Don't forget. Drive slowly and carefully. Drop the bike off and get to the RDZ. Do not screw up now. You have done great so far. OK?"

"Sure," said Jon relieved. Sweat was dripping down his face and Surge thought he looked ten years older.

Surge walked quickly into the tube station. The Grey Man had explained exactly where the CCTV cameras were and as he passed them he pulled on the brim of his cap and kept his head down. The tube train looked like it was waiting for him as he walked straight on and then travelled across London, sitting quietly calling off the stops in his mind. His body was pumped with adrenalin but he was fully under control. This was his life, and he felt so alive.

At the other end, Surge jogged up the stairs and saw Collins sitting there in the driving seat of a black London cab. As Surge jumped in, Collins switched the meter to 'On Hire' and smoothly drove off. Surge took off the cap and jumper and reached below the seat. He pulled out some clothes and put on a long blue raincoat with a leather collar and changed his trainers for smart leather brogues. He also put on a pair of heavy rimmed glasses with clear lenses.

"Everything OK?" said Collins.

"Sure," replied Surge. "So far a piece of cake."

"How about Jon?" asked Collins.

"Terrific. A chip off the old block," said Surge giving Collins one of his rare smiles.

Collins physically relaxed. Two minutes later they had arrived and Collins pulled over as Surge got out and paid. Collins said quietly

"No heroics Surge, OK?"

Surge was about to say something facetious until he saw the concern in the older man's eyes.

"Don't worry. I will not fight him." he said.

Collins flipped the 'Not For Hire' sign. He pulled out a flask and made a show of pouring coffee for all the world to see his was on a break. Surge walked over to the alley and got out his mobile pretending to make a call. Both felt self-conscious and hoped they blended in.

Exactly on time a dark blue 3 series BMW slowly drove up with two men inside. Surge could see it was Mickey and the Bull. As always Mickey parked on the yellow line opposite the restaurant. They both sat quietly scanning the street. Neither appeared to take any notice of Collins or Surge. After a couple of minutes the Bull got out of the car and Collins held his breath at the size of the man. At least 6ft 5inches tall, broad of back with massive arms covered in tattoos. He moved well, Collins thought, looking like a born athlete. Collins eyes flicked to Surge who had also started moving. The timing was critical. The Bull was normally in the restaurant for just a few seconds expecting the package to be ready. Mickey sat quietly, eyes focused looking through the windscreen, as the Bull disappeared into the shop and the door closed.

Surge put his hand in his coat pocket and wrapped his fist around the koboken. He moved forward checking that he stayed in Mickey's blind spot. As he came along side the car his arm swept sideways, the point hit the safety glass cleanly and smashed straight through with barely a sound, just the glass falling to the pavement. Surge continued moving forward bending and twisting, extending his arm, the koboken hitting Mickey hard directly on the soft spot on the side of his temple. The thin bone broke and blood spurted out in a pulsing stream. Mickey passed out immediately and shot onto his side with the force of the blow, his head now in the passenger well, unconscious, possibly dead.

The Bull had got into the restaurant and as his hand grabbed the package he had one eye on the long mirror above the counter covering the car in the road outside. It was why Mickey always parked in the same spot so the Bull could keep an eye on him while Mickey scanned the area for the Bull. He saw Surge walk up swing his arm through the car window and Mickey disappear. He turned with a rage and rushed out the door shouting. Surge straightened up and saw the Bull flying towards him. He calmly walked in front of the car moving to the centre of the road blocking Collins view and gesturing him covertly with his left hand not to do anything.

The Assassin Collins opened the car door and stepped out. His hand was in his jacket on the gun handle. He had no need to pull it out and point it. If the shot was there he would draw aim and shoot in one smooth move but Surge was in the way.

The Bull raced towards the middle-aged man who was standing calmly waiting. He was livid but in control, fighting was his life and this old man would be destroyed for hurting Mickey. Collins watched with dread as the Bull rushed towards Surge, arms up like a wrestler. Surge merely stood in the middle of the road, straddling the white line, his knees slightly bent, one foot in front of the other pointing at ten to two on a clock face, his arms by his side. It looked like a classic martial art stance that you would perform in a dojo, not a stance you would pull in a street fight. As the Bull closed the distance, he lunged, landing lightly on his right foot, pivoting on the ball and sending a right hook with all the power he could muster. Had it landed it would have taken Surge's head off. As it was, Surge lent back as the punch swung towards him and shot out his left leg with the foot still angled at 10 o'clock. It was not a kick, more of a stamp that dislocated the Bull's right kneecap detaching it fully from its bed of gristle and it twisted up his thigh muscle. The Bull's right hook whistled by Surge's chin by a whisker and as the Bull, by now off balance, started to collapse under his weakened right leg, Surge stepped to the right and stiffening the fingers of his left hand he jabbed powerfully into the Bull's throat crushing it at the base. The Bull dropped to the ground, a mute scream on his face as air could neither get in or out. He lashed around dying as Surge picked up the third parcel and walked calmly over to the taxi climbing into the back seat.

Collins drove off as fast as the taxi would go, twisting and turning down the lanes. He turned to Surge, livid, his face showing his concern, red with temper.

"You bastard! You told me you were not going to fight him. You promised me!"

Surge looked back, calmly settled himself in the seat and said, "I didn't fight him. I broke him. That's what I do."

Collins changed cars dropping off the taxi in a back alley and they both got into a grey Audi A6, neither spoke again, then he dropped Surge off close to his flat. It was still only mid-afternoon but Surge felt drained as he always did after action. He lay on his small bed and dozed. He awoke feeling better and ate a light meal and then wondered whether to go to the gym. Pru would be there he had already said goodbye to her but The Grey Man had told him to carry on as normal and secretly he knew he wanted to see her one last time. Surge changed, slung his bag across his shoulder and jogged to the gym. It was past work hours now and he knew she would have been there a while. As usual her face lit up when she saw him and they started on their round of stretching and exercises together, both knowing this would probably be their last night together at least for a while. Surge felt a strange feeling sweeping over him, in that moment, a cross between happiness and contentment, not something he was used to. He had performed well today, better than expected, and also enjoyed just being around Pru. He felt reborn, fitter and stronger than he had been for years. Maybe life was going to be OK from now on. Finally Surge might had found some stability in his life. But what happens tomorrow? he thought. The mission was nearly over. Would he be happy going back to the books and the beer? He just didn't know.

One person who wasn't happy was the Stinger. He arrived with a face like thunder. The word went round that he had failed a drugs test and was now banned from boxing for two years. Surge was not surprised. He had seen him inject himself in the changing room to enhance his training, the steroid allowing him to train longer and harder. Silly boy, Surge had thought. So much natural talent wasted.

The Stinger changed and started to strut around obviously looking for a fight, flicking punches at anyone he walked past, daring the other boxers to step up. Someone was going to get hurt today, he thought. Finally The Stinger came to Surge. The old man had always pissed him off. Sure the Stinger had caught him a few but he was a messer, never letting the Stinger look good, all elbows and arms and off balance. He decided a lesson was to be taught.

"Oi! Punchy," he shouted. "Get in the ring now."

Surge sensed the mood. The last thing he wanted today was trouble. He tried to decline but the Stinger pushed him in the chest.

"Either in the ring or out of it. Your choice, you piece of shit," he said.

Pru tried to interfere. "Leave him alone," she said, but he just pushed harder and reluctantly, trying to avoid a scene, Surge stepped into the ring.

There were no preliminaries. The Stinger shot across the ring throwing full power left and rights. Surge did his best to cover up but this kid meant business, he thought. The Stringer was young, strong and fast and blows rained down. Surge no longer did his training dance, just tried to cover up.

Pru was shouting, "Stop this! Stop this!" but everyone ignored her as the Stinger threw the rule book to the wind and unloaded bomb after bomb, no longer boxing, almost going berserk. Blood was coming from Surge's nose, mouth and ears. So far no real damage but Surge was starting to get desperate. He couldn't break the boy in front of everyone but also he could not take much more before he got seriously hurt.

Finally the trainer walked over, rang the bell and shouted to the Stinger. "OK, OK," he said. "He has had enough. Leave him alone."

Surge dropped to one knee pulling off the boxing gloves as the Stinger, arms aloft danced round him.

"Get up! Get up you coward!" he jeered. "You are nothing, you old bastard!"

Pru had seen enough. She jumped into the ring and pushed the Stinger in the chest.

"Back off!" she shouted.

"Or what?" said the Stinger. "What are you going to do, you dried up dyke?"

Pru snapped. First years of taunts from her husband, now Mark getting a beating. She planted her feet and threw a sharp right cross just as she had been trained to do. It almost landed but the Stinger was a professional boxer, at the top of his game. He swayed back and the punch whistled by. He then backhanded her with his left and was about to follow it with a nasty right hook. It never landed. Surge swept up from his knees blocking the blow by punching up and into the crooked elbow breaking the joint. Then as part of the same move his right elbow smashed into the Stinger's face breaking his jaw and three teeth. Surge reversed his arm and wrapped it round the Stinger's neck, pulling him down as his knee came up breaking the cheek bones and, as the Stinger's body jerked upward from the knee strike, Surge let him go then punched down, breaking two ribs.

Finally in one flowing move he kicked out shattering the ankle joint and sweeping the Stinger's legs away. He dropped down senseless. In all, the one flowing move had taken part of a second and afterwards no one could quite describe what had happened. One minute the Stinger was in charge, the next he was in pieces on the canvas.

Surge looked around and felt another emotion that was alien to him – rage. He could not remember when he had last lost control like this but this bastard had tried to hit Pru. He looked around.

"Anyone else?" he shouted. "ANYONE?" No one caught his eye.

Pru grabbed him. She pulled him from the ring as the other boxers stood around the Stinger. Then she ran to the changing rooms, grabbed both their bags.

"Let's go," she said.

On the street he calmed down and they walked in silence. After a while she reached out and held his hand.

"Are you OK?" she said.

"Fine. I couldn't let him hit you Pru," he said.

"I know," she said.

"I have led you into danger and that is unforgivable," said Surge.

"Do you think they will come after us?" she said, looking over her shoulder.

"No, not them. But others much more deadly."

They walked on. Surge's mind spinning. How long before they put together the day's hits and him breaking the boxer. It would not be difficult to connect. Would they give him this one day? That's all they needed to find and take out the top men. London was a big place. Surely it would take time to filter through.

Pru found a pub and Surge sat down in the corner. She went to the bar and not knowing what to order, bought two brandies to steady their nerves. She sat down and he reached across and took her hand.

"Pru, I am in a lot of trouble," he said. "Some heavy weight guys are hunting me down. I cannot tell you why but because of what just happened in the gym they will find you. I need you to disappear. Can you do that?"

"Why will they come after me?" she said.

"Because you are a link to me, one step nearer to finding me and these guys are professionals, they will not hold back."

Pru looked deep into his eyes. "What then?" she said.

"I will find you," said Surge.

"But you won't know where I have gone," said Pru.

"Trust me," he said. "There is nowhere in this world where I cannot find you."

"Why would you want to?" she said.

As she asked the question a wave of emotion hit him as if his heart had opened up for the first time in his life.

"Because," he said. "I love you and will give you a new life if you will have me." He was more shocked by the words than she was, but he knew what he had said was the truest statement he had ever made.

Her eyes misted up. She had known all along they were destined for each other it had just taken him some time to catch up. She started to tell him about her life, the good and the bad telling him everything she thought he would need to understand her. She said she would make a good wife, told him of her dreams of children and a home, of happiness and security. He listened, holding her hand and gazing into her eyes, the drinks forgotten.

At closing time, he walked her home and she asked him in, both knowing it was a loaded question.

"No," he said. "Next time, when we are really together." He looked deep into her eyes pleading with her. "You must disappear Pru?" he begged. "It is very important."

"I promise," she said. "First train out in the morning. How long before I see you again?"

"Give me a few weeks, a month at most," he said and she kissed him and watched him walk away.

He wandered out into the night, his thoughts in turmoil and kept on walking not wanting to go back to his flat. He thought about the day and especially Pru. Where to start again, Canada or the USA? He had plenty of money. The Grey Man would help with passports, visa etc, and they could start a new life, somewhere open with fields and space and he thought of children and how he would give them a different childhood to his. As he walked along the Surgeon started to disappear and the man came through. He no longer wanted a life of loneliness and violence. 'I want to be normal,' he thought. 'Just get through tomorrow and see.' For the first time in years the world held possibilities.

As he walked, his mind drifted and he found himself early in the morning at a church that had finished a midnight service and was still open so he wandered in and sat on a pew, crossing his arms and resting his head on the back of the pew in front. It had been a long time since he had talked to his God. He opened his heart and confessed his sins, something that had been a long time in coming and then unburdened, he fell into a deep sleep.

He was awakened in the early morning by a kindly priest.

"Are you OK my son?" he asked.

"I think so Father," said Surge smiling and walked out into the light. He looked at his watch and realised Jon would be picking him up soon. He started to jog home, bag across his back. 'Shower and shave,' he thought. Then he would tell The Grey Man and Collins about the boxer.

Chapter 17

Lee was having a bad day. The world was falling around his ears. The phone had not stopped ringing. He had been threatened, sworn at and screamed at. However after two hours of frantic negotiations, he had kept it all together. Just. Each gang that had been hit, he sent £100k to the leader and £10k to the guy that had been hit. To the Bull's family, he sent a further £100k. This had calmed things down a bit and with the leaders a bit richer and slightly mollified, he had been told he had 48 hours to sort this out or there would be a war. His head was to be the first trophy.

Lee sat in a huge leather chair in his elegant apartment looking out of the window as darkness descended. Everything pointed to the gang that had not been hit but he just did not buy it, too simple , too pat. Who could have done this? Who had the kind of organisation able to take him on? His thoughts went to John Sea. Had he said too much? Was Sea muscling in? As if on cue his mobile rang.

"John Sea here ," said the deadpan voice. "I have heard you had a bit of trouble."

"Nothing I cannot handle," said Lee. "Was it you?"

John Sea laughed. "If it had been me," he said "You would be dead."

"Who then?" asked Lee.

"I have heard a whisper," he said. "No more than that from a very old friend in the Secret Service who provides various services. There are three men hunting you."

"Only three?" said Lee. "Surely not."

"I know of these men," said Sea. "And let me tell you this. If the whisper I heard said I was the target I would be gone, packed and on the next plane out. Do you understand?"

"I am not you," said Lee. "I do not give up easily."

"So," said Sea. "I have more choices for you. Run and lose everything or stay and fight against an enemy you do not know or can even guess how dangerous they are."

"I stay," said Lee.

"OK," said Sea. "Let's put this down as a test. If you and your organisation are around in one month from today we have a deal. OK?"

"Sure," said Lee. "Any more info you can give me about my problem?"

"Only that these men are not after your money or your organisation. They are trying to bring you down. It's a matter of honour. Look to the shadows," said Sea and the line went dead.

Lee put down the phone and was in a much better mood. No conspiracy, no double-cross from the organisation but an outside force muscling in. This he could handle. He called Smith and filled him in on the call from Sea.

"Mick, I want a £50k reward to any man who can find out anything. These must be players and will be on someone's radar. Find a firm that's trying to get in our back yard. Look for anything out of the ordinary. These hits were professional and talent is always known. Also the hits yesterday show a detailed level of intelligence on the movements of our people. No question. The operation have been watched and studied. Talk to the receivers to see if they have spotted anyone who might have been asking questions or hanging around. Finally back track over every place we have visited in the last three months. Look for someone who wants revenge."

Peter Lee was galvanised into action. This was better. He now knew he had a foe and who would find them. London was full of part time and full time villains and many would sell their mothers for £50k. The people who were after him would get a shock at how far his reach extended.

He drove to the restaurant where Bull was killed and had the owner take him into his office. He first checked that the man had said nothing to the police, once satisfied, ascertained that when Bull had run out of the shop the owner had followed. Lee made him tell his story .

"I saw a man walk to the white line in the road, a big man but not as big as the Bull. Not a young man either, forty maybe fifty, maybe older," he said calmly.

"Bollocks," said Lee. "I do not believe you. The Bull was in his prime. No old man could have taken him. How long was the fight?"

"Two seconds," said the owner laughing. "And the man made it look easy, so sweet, like slapping a child."

Lee grabbed the owner by his jacket collar and punched him twice in the face, two vicious jabs. "Look you bastard, don't fucking snow me!"

The owner looked at him scared, blood running from his nose.

"I promise," he said shaking. "The man just kicked out and the Bull started to fall. Then he hit him in the throat."

"What then?" said Lee.

"He walked over to a taxi that was waiting for him and they drove away. I have the licence number."

They talked for a few more minutes, Lee trying to get better descriptions of the man and taxi driver. Lee wrote down everything including the registration number of the cab. He called Smith and gave him the description. He then phoned an associate at DVLA who told him the licence plate was false.

Lee drove back to the apartment, his mind spinning on the day's results. He sat there drinking without tasting a 10 year old single malt, waiting for the phone to ring. Nothing happened, as hours dragged by. This was impossible. Someone must know something. Finally at midnight he took a call from Smith.

"It is quiet," said Smith. "No firm moving, no one talking. Only one bit of strangeness that might fit. An old man they called Punchy, beat up Steve the Stinger in a gym. Apparently, went through him like a dose of salts. Big man, early fifties. Of any interest?"

"Yes," screamed Lee, jumping to his feet. "I knew it. They always fuck up. Where's this gym?"

Smith gave him the address.

"Meet me there in 20 minutes," said Lee. "And bring the manager of the place."

Lee sat at the managers desk, down in a dingy back room of the gym. In front of him he had Pru's and Mark Emblem's addresses. Pru had paid with a credit card and Lee had already had a contact run that information. Mark Emblem paid cash.

"They called the guy Punchy," said the manager. "For the past few months he has been training here most days. All different hours, pushing himself hard."

"What type of training?" asked Smith.

"Mainly heavy bag. Skipping, sparring, weights. Sometimes I have seen him on the dojo floor, going through weird routines."

"Like what?" said Lee.

"A martial art kata, but very awkward, real strange. He moves well for his age, perfect with bag and skipping rope, until he gets in the ring. Then he cannot fight at all. Everyone beats him. He moves so strangely. Perfect in the gym, then useless in the ring. That's why they call him Punchy but truth to tell, few hits landed cleanly when he boxed. He is an awkward cuss, all arms and elbows and off balance,".

"So tell me about the fight with the Stinger?" said Smith.

"Hey man, that was no fight," said the manager. "Punchy just steps up and the next thing the Stinger is in a ball at his feet. The man just took him apart as if he was nothing."

Smith and Lee exchanged glances. "And the girl?"

"Nothing much to say. She's been coming here for some time. Then she starts to get close to Punchy and they start training together. She is obviously keen on him. He gets into the ring with the Stinger who is in a bad mood and starts to unload on Punchy. She gets into a slanging match and the Stinger gives her a slap. That's when Punchy does him."

Lee handed over a wad of cash.

"If he comes back, call me," he said. "And we haven't been here. Right?"

"Sure, sure," says the manager.

By the time Lee and Smith walked out from the gym to the pavement, it's around 1.00am.

"I want this sorted now," said Lee. "Find them! Get every bit of information. Who? What? Why? And then chop them up! Take the three boys and get the Jamaican. This guy is dangerous."

"I can take him," says Smith.

"Sure," says Lee. "But why take the chance? Send in the Jamaican. It's his manor and then follow-up. OK? No unnecessary risks."

Chapter 18

Surge jogged up the stairs to his flat and along the dingy landing. As he opened the door a smell wafted through. He had smelt it so many times before. Blood and the stink of excrement from when the bowels open. Death. He inched his way along the narrow corridor towards the front room and dipped his head around the corner before stopping dead. In front of him tied to a chair was Pru. She was seated to give the maximum shock. Blouse ripped open, throat slashed. Blood had poured down her front, down her legs onto the floor. Her face had been beaten badly and one of her arms was at an unnatural angle. Obviously the bone was broken. She had been tortured before being killed.

The blood drained from his face. Tears filled his eyes and he almost collapsed. A man used to death he had never felt so emotionally out of control. His soul wept, the life he had dreamt of just a few hours ago ripped cruelly away and it was his fault she had been murdered.

"Oh Pru," he cried "what have I done?"

Suddenly Surge felt a sharp pain in his back, pushing him into the room. He turned round. A huge Jamaican man was blocking the corridor, long dreadlocks, wearing a brown suit with a white open collar shirt and carrying a razor sharp machete.

"She gave the right address at the gym, man, unlike you, but didn't know nothing man," he said in a low voice. "Except for this place where she had followed you one night. Screamed and screamed but said nothing. But you know everything and are going to tell me, right?"

Surge stepped back into the room and looked around.

"Nowhere to run man," said the Jamaican.

"Who wants to run?" said Surge coldly, as his right foot flicked out hitting the wrist that held the machete which spun from the Jamaican's hand. Surge completed the move by crouching down and spinning on the ball of his left foot, dropping flat to the floor, his right leg extended and sweeping the man's legs from under him causing his head to hit the wall of the narrow corridor. He fell painfully to his knees. Surge now sprung up into a crouch. His left arm went across the Jamaican's throat, the right arm across his neck. He joined hands and clamped down the scissor action causing enormous pressure on the windpipe and the Jamaican clawed at Surge's arm trying to breathe and to get to his feet. Surge flipped himself over the man's back in a tumbler's roll while still clamping hard, levering with his whole strength and weight. The fulcrum of the lever was the Jamaican's neck and as Surge reached the nine o'clock position, the force was unbearable and a large crack sounded through the flat. The Jamaican now looked unnaturally far over his right shoulder, his neck broken and he dropped to the floor dead.

Surge released the hold and rolled to his feet. He stepped back into the room and for a second looked down at Pru.

"Sorry," was all he could think to say. He picked up the phone and dialled The Firm.

"Two to clean and a flat to fumigate," he said and hung up, then dialled a code which would alert Collins and The Grey Man they were compromised. He cursed. It was his fault.

Surge went out onto the landing his mind spinning with possibilities. Then his heart dropped Jon must be outside he thought. Would they know him? he moved quickly putting all the dreams he had planned with Pru behind him marked as just another failure in his life. His face was set, grim. No trace of the man left. The Surgeon was back.

He ran down the steps into a grey dingy wet morning and spotted them immediately as they did him. Two approached from the right, two from the left, all big men, all hard looking. Good but not professional. Professionals would have been closer together. He could use that. He spotted Jon's car and started to walk quickly towards it. If he could catch the two on the right napping, lagging behind ,he could break the two on the left before they could get to him, then run to Jon's car and be off.

Jon sat in the car waiting. He saw Surge come down the stairs and the four men appear. It was obvious who they were after. He knew Surge was good, but not that good. Even he could not fight four such big men. He had to even the odds. Jon opened the car door and in a crouch ran across the road keeping low. He saw Surge hurry towards the nearest two men and Jon charged. He had never fought in his life so he took the biggest man in a low flying rugby tackle, just like he had at university and knocked the big man from his feet but the other man was faster. Surge had started to run as he saw Jon move but the smaller man had pulled a gun and now held it to Jon's head.

"One move and I will kill him," he said. Surge was still ten paces away and stopped.

"Hands on your head," said the man and Surge complied. The big man got up, turned and kicked Jon full in the face.

"That's for starters," he said. They pushed and dragged Surge and Jon to a big black Mercedes.

Smith caught up to them. He threw Jon and Surge face first against the car and searched them. He took out both mobile phones, turned them off and threw them in the back seat of the car.

He recognised Jon from the surveillance he had done on the shop before approaching and then killing his mother.

"What are you doing in all this?" he demanded. Jon just looked at him insolently and Smith punched him hard in the gut doubling him over. He called Lee and explained about Jon.

"This does not make sense," he said. "I checked the boy and his mother out. Both clean. He is just a student, not part of an underworld gang. What do you want me to do with them?"

"Bring them to the farmhouse," said Lee. "I want to get to the bottom of this."

He put the phone down and said to himself, 'John Sea said vengeance, but a shopkeeper's wife? This cannot be right.'

Surge and Jon were bundled into the boot of the S class Mercedes. As they drove, Surge wriggled round till he could whisper into Jon's ear.

"Do not say anything," he said. "As soon as you tell them anything, you are dead. Your father is coming and trust me, when he catches up, these shits are all dead. Hold out for as long as you can. Understand?"

Jon nodded in the dark of the boot. He was shaking with fear and did not trust himself to speak.

Chapter 19

Collins called and spoke to The Grey Man. Something had gone wrong. He had received the warning code from Surge and now both Surge's phone and Jon's were turned off.

"Give me five minutes," said The Grey Man and hung up. The Grey Man put a call into The Firm and heard about the clean up at Surge's flat. How were we compromised, he worried? The girl was a mystery. Surge was not a man to fool about with women especially on a mission. He switched on his computer and after a few screens picked up Surge's phone on GPS heading into the south of England towards Eastbourne. Even though the phones were off, The Grey Man still had a transponder active on both. He called Collins back and filled him in.

"We need to follow them as quickly as possible," said Collins. "Pick me up on your way through."

"Ten minutes," said The Grey Man.

As he set down the phone a wave of remorse and worry swept through Collins. First he had lost his wife and now because of him his son was in mortal danger, but he put it aside. He was The Assassin. All his life he had dealt with the eventuality of death either his own or someone else's. Whatever happened, as God was his witness, he would have his vengeance today.

Collins went upstairs into the master bedroom in the old house. Opposite the en-suite was a set of wardrobe doors and a small dressing area. He went to the back wall and twisted a hidden bracket which allowed the wall to hinge towards him revealing a long thin room. He had made the room himself when they moved in and this space had become his workshop. Lined all along the walls on neat shelves were the tools of his trade, by category - sniper rifles, machine guns of all sizes from military through to uzis and a wall full of hand pistols. The last he had the most of, in all ranges and sizes, all immaculately maintained. In the corner was a selection of holsters. He picked up one small holster in black leather connected to a black webbing belt which went round his waist with the holster nestling high on his right hip. He inspected the lining and then from a small pot rubbed in some black chalk. He then took down a small modern looking hand gun and tried it in the holster, smoothly putting it in and out until he was satisfied with the movement.

Before walking over to the bench and laying the gun on the green soft baize. In a number of quick deft movements he stripped it, inspected the spring, barrel and trigger movement, oiled where it was needed and reassembled it. Then put the gun and holster to one side.

He next selected a large old holster on straps which he pulled down from the wall. It was designed to go round his back, over his shoulder and the holster to end up under his right armpit for a left hand draw. The holster and strap were also black leather, much used but still in good condition, the leather now as soft as butter. He after some indecision, pulled down a huge handgun. It was a design from the 1970's and used by the LAPD motor cycle cops for shooting through car engines to get the bad guys to stop. It was called the elephant pistol. Hugely heavy, unwieldy and hard to control, because of this it was taken out of service soon after it was introduced and was now quite rare. He stripped, oiled and rebuilt the gun and put it to one side near the smaller one he had selected earlier with boxes of ammo for both. For the big gun he had selected illegal dum dum bullets designed to shatter on hitting the target. It would make a small hole on entry then explode leaving a huge exit hole. If someone was shot in the arm, then very little of the arm would be left. Any shot to head or body was always fatal.

He walked back to the closet and selected a leather Gladstone bag. From the bathroom he took a selection of towels, lay one at the bottom of the bag and wrapped both guns, ammo and holsters in the others before also putting them into the bag. Next he changed into his work outfit. Soft rubber soled black shoes, black trousers and belt and a black cotton shirt and windcheater. The bulkiness of the windcheater would mask even the elephant pistol.

He heard a screech of tyres on the gravel and rushed downstairs. The Grey Man was there in a powerful dark blue A8 4.2 litre Audi. He got out swiftly and opened the boot to allow The Assassin to put in his Gladstone bag, then passed him the keys.

"You drive. I will navigate," he said.

The Assassin got in the driver's seat and buckled up.

"How long do you think they have been gone?" he asked.

"Fifty minutes to an hour, tops. I know where they are heading," replied The Grey Man. "We can get there at around the same time as they arrive if we are lucky."

"How do you know where they are going?" said Collins.

"Well, somehow we screwed up but also got lucky. Last night the criminal underground lit up with a £50k contract for any news on Surge. I chased the contract back to a Mr Peter Lee and ran a full background check, phone, bank, etc. A man who likes to live the high life but always in the background, very clever, I would think the top man running the organisation. He has a sidekick called Smith, a real thug and probably the man you met in the shop. Probably the man who killed your wife as he likes to do the dirty work himself. There is also our crooked money man called Stevens and lots of contacts. All quite ruthless. I can map the full network now."

"Lee recently purchased a farmhouse near Hastings and that is almost certainly where they are going. I see no major contacts outside the criminal fraternity so no complications getting rid of him, but he has been talking to an old friend, John Sea."

"That bastard!" said The Assassin. "What's he involved for?"

"Not sure," said The Grey Man. "I think our Lee was fishing in Sea's pond and has been warned off."

Collins drove fast but competently, no flashy turns or screeching of tyres, as always from the outside he looked completely in control but his mind was spinning. Once this was over, Israel for him and Jon, he thought. No more of this. He would buy some land and revisit his roots, sit in the sunshine and drink some wine. A brief image settled in his mind of Jon beaten and broken and he hit the accelerator harder, flashing through a red light and setting off a number of speed cameras. The Grey Man sat there in silence holding on for dear life as corners came and went at dizzying speed. He just hoped they did not pass a police car. They had no time to evade, lose and transfer to a new car but their luck held and the miles passed by.

Surge, from the confines of the boot, heard the crackle of gravel as they pulled onto the drive and then stopped. He whispered to Jon, "Be strong" as the boot opened and the light streamed in. Their eyes locked and Surge could see the fear there. He smiled and winked. One man stepped back brandishing a shot gun. another grabbed Jon by the collar and hair dragging him from the boot and throwing him to the ground. Surge managed to clamber out by himself which bought him a savage punch to the stomach from Smith, which doubled him over, and left and right punchs to the face which knocked him to the ground. The front door was pulled open on the old farmhouse and both men were dragged into the hall and then through to the large back room. In the corner was a desk with a smart looking man sitting behind it working on a laptop. Seats were placed in front of it, which is where Jon and Surge were thrown.

Lee got up from the desk and walked round. Smith was to the right with the two big men standing at the back of the room. The man with the shotgun walked to the corner to get coverage of the room with his gun. He pointed it at the floor but was able to straighten and fire instantly if needed. Lee ignored Surge who just sat there looking down and walked up to Jon who defiantly looked him in the eyes.

"What is this all about?" demanded Lee.

"You killed my mother," said Jon.

Surge sent him a sharp look and Jon went quiet.

"So fucking what?" shouted Smith. "She was a mouthy bitch who got what she asked for."

Jon went mad and leapt out of the chair. He was grabbed by Lee and Smith hit him with a powerful lazy right hand punch which caught Jon high on the head and knocked him to the floor. Smith then followed up with a number of kicks and punches to Jon's face and body which went on for some time. Jon was bleeding from nose and mouth and both started to swell up. Surge went to move but the man with the shotgun moved forward a pace and levelled the gun.

Smith dragged the semi conscious Jon back to the chair.

Jon managed to look up. "Fuck you," he said defiantly, with tears and blood running down his face.

Smith steamed in again before Lee told him to stop. Jon slumped in the chair and Lee gave him a second to recover.

"Brave lad," Lee said to Surge. "But soft. Not one of us."

He walked back to the desk and opened a draw from which he pulled a small hand gun. He made a show of loading it from a box of bullets and cocked it. He walked back. Looking Jon in the eye and without looking away, calmly shot Surge in the leg just above the knee. Surge cried out and Jon screamed in shock and frustration, his voice echoing with the sound of the gun.

"Let's start again," Lee said to Jon. "I only need one of you and unless you start cooperating I will kill this man a piece at time." With that he held the gun to Surge's shoulder. Blood was running from Surge's leg down his trousers making a small pool on the floor.

"OK," said Jon and Surge looked away. "My dad is coming for you. After you shot my mother he went mad. He has some friends in the police who have helped him find you and Surge here is an ex-boxer."

"Where is your father now?" said Lee.

"Probably at home," said Jon. "Waiting for me to call. He has money and I am sure would pay you to get us back."

"I don't believe you," said Smith. "The operation yesterday was too slick." He gestured at Surge. "If it wasn't for this moron getting the hots for a piece at the gym, we would never have found you. Try again."

"OK, OK," said Jon, desperate tears streaming down his face. "My dad was in the army in Israel and he knows a thing or two, that's all. It is just him, Surge and me. Honest."

"Did you get a message to him when you saw us earlier?" asked Lee. "No," said Jon.

"He is lying," said Smith. "He is stalling for time. I wonder why?"

"Hold on Mick," said Lee. "Look at him. He is not a professional. He is crapping himself. Would you take a boy like this into a fight with us? No, so let's assume this story is true. Let's be honest, there has not been one report coming back of any known firm looking into us, no indication of any large operation, so let's assume he is kosher. I bet he called his dad the first sign of danger and I bet his dad has the brains to track us so he will be coming here. If so, we get the chance to kill him. If not, we hunt him down and kill him at home. Job done! Keep the boy alive. I am sure his dad will tell us everything he knows with a gun to his son's head."

He looked at Smith. "We only need one. Get rid of this piece of shit," he said looking at Surge. Smith reached for his gun. "Not here! There is enough blood on my carpets. Take him to the garage."

Smith turned to the two big guys lounging against the wall and said,

"This turd thinks he is a hard man, a fighter. Well, live by the sword, die by the sword. Take him to the garage and beat him to death." He motioned to the man with the shotgun. "Keep him covered."

He then turned to Lee, "I will stay with you and we can wait for his old man to show."

The two big men grabbed Surge by the arm and dragged him into the hall and out through the front door. Jon had wanted to say something but could not think of anything. The pain from the beating washed over him. Had he given his dad away? They were waiting for him now. Two frightening criminals, both armed were waiting for his dad - the little Jewish businessman who Jon had never seen lose his temper or raise his voice, who loved him and his mother, and who was now walking into certain death because of him. He had to do something, but what?

The Assassin and The Grey Man parked the car out of sight and looked through the hedge at the large farmhouse. Nothing stirred. The strong morning sunlight filtered through the leaves. It was a beautiful day. The birds were singing and the smell of the country was strong. My boy is in there, thought Collins, probably being tortured. A shot rang out and both men feared the worst. They walked back to the car. Collins opened the boot. He stripped of the jacket and opened the Gladstone bag. He passed the belt round his waist and steadied the holster at his right hip. He pulled out the smaller gun, checked the mechanism, loaded it and slipped it into the holster. He then strapped on the shoulder holster settling it under his right armpit, checked and loaded the big gun which he slipped into the waiting holster. He then flexed and resettled both holsters until they hung just right, all done smoothly and unhurried. He stepped back and closed the boot.

The Grey Man was transfixed. He had just seen a human chameleon, a man change into another man in front of his face. Not just because the guns were in place, now there was a complete change of attitude and purpose. In front of him was a black clad stranger. Nothing of the shopkeeper was left, just a grim faced killer. The Assassin stepped forward and they moved swiftly back to the hedge just in time to see Surge being dragged out of the front door. "See what you can do for him" he said, "I will get Jon" and without a backward glance he started a circular route round the house hugging the hedge to get closer.

Surge's mind was racing. He could feel the blood running down his leg and the strength flowing from him. Twice now he had manoeuvred one or the other of the thugs between him and the man with the shotgun but the man was quick, constantly finding the kill line. With Surge's leg leaking blood he just could not move fast enough. He knew once he was in the garage they would come for him and he would have to act, hopefully taking at least one of these bastards with him. He could see no other way.

As he was dragged through the front door his eye scanned the undergrowth and he found what he was looking for - movement in the hedge, and his heart soared. It must be Collins and The Grey Man he thought. He knew they would not be far behind. If I can just hold on for a few more minutes, he thought. His mind flew to the beating in Northern Ireland and remarkably he found he was not scared any more. He realised that the fear he had known for the past five years was due to him being unconscious when he had been beaten and waking up paralysed. Here he would look these bastards in the eye, Ireland no longer haunted him. It never would again. He could face this and if needed, would go down fighting.

The garage door was flung open and Surge thrown the length of it. The door was closed and the light switched on.

"Think you are a hard bastard?" said one of the thugs. "I'll have you screaming like your little bitch girlfriend." With the gunman covering him, he rushed at Surge throwing punches right and left in a frenzy. Surge dodged and moved as best he could but the blows rained down on him. He could feel his cheekbone break and then a few ribs. Once the thug had started to breathe hard he stepped back and the other man moved forward keeping up the punishment. Blood flowed all down Surge's face and he felt his body break.

The Grey Man had worked his way round to the side door and looked through the glass. All three men were riveted on the beating Surge was taking. The Grey Man expertly and silently picked the lock and gently prised the door open. He had never learnt to fight as that would have meant bodily contact, something he could not stand and he worried what to do. One old man against three was suicide but he would not stand by and let Surge be beaten to death. He waited until he was sure no one was looking in his direction, held his breath and then charged the man with the shotgun spinning it from his hand and knocking them both to the ground. He found himself on top but the man was younger, fitter and stronger. He rolled The Grey Man over and The Grey Man looked back at Surge and wished he hadn't. The two men beating Surge had turned round when The Grey Man had pounced and then when they saw it was no problem, turned back to their beating, but now they saw a different animal and The Grey Man saw what the men saw. With no gun to cover him Surge was free. His eyes were the eyes of the devil as he glided up from the floor, something hideous and bloody and mean, filled with rage and purpose, something that exuded hate and bile. Unstoppable.

The Grey Man had to look away as he was caught with a vicious punch by his assailant who now sat astride his chest pinning him down and preparing to let loose with right and left punches. But before he could settle himself, the man stopped in shock when he heard a noise, not made by anything human, then a curious whimper followed by the smack of something hard hitting flesh, then the smell of bowels opening. The Grey Man had no idea what Surge had done and didn't ever want to know but both of the big men were now in the foetal position on the floor lying in pools of their own bodily fluids, slowly dying, their faces contorted in the most abject agony as if Surge had ripped the very souls from their bodies.

The Grey Man's opponent sensing the danger went to rise but The Grey Man grabbed his arms holding them tight with all his strength. Surge painfully rose to his feet and fell towards them kicking out with his right leg and casually breaking the man's neck, killing him instantly.

The Grey Man looked up into Surge's eyes and for a second they locked before Surge's eyes dimmed and he collapsed onto to the dusty grey cement floor.

"No!" shouted The Grey Man and he did something he had never done before, something he thought he was not capable of, he reached out and embraced Surge. His arms went around him and he hugged him close. He looked down, tears falling from his eyes onto Surge's face. "Don't die," he said softly. "Don't die," but there was no movement and The Grey Man, looking through his tears, thought he was gone.

Then Surge sucked in a shallow breath and then a large one as he came back, his eyes opened and something passed between the two men, love, friendship, two lonely souls who recognised in each other a kindred spirit.

"Get me to the boy," whispered Surge. "I promised Collins I would look after him and this is all my fault." The Grey Man wiped his eyes and carefully helped Surge to his feet and half dragged, half carried, the badly injured heavier man towards the house.

The Assassin worked his way round the house and in through the open front door. He could hear voices talking softly when one rung out in a cultured Oxbridge tone obviously loud enough for The Assassin to hear, "Won't you come in?"

He swung the door open and walked into a large elegantly furnished room at the back of the house. Jon was sitting on a chair facing him, bolt upright and looking completely dishevelled and beaten, with dried blood on his face. But alive. Behind him was a smartly dressed man who had a gun to Jon's head. To his left lounging against the wall was the man who had come into the shop and had hit him.

Smith laughed. "Tell me this is not true," he said out loud. "This tired old Jew has caused all the problems. Lee wasn't laughing. He looked at the guns The Assassin was carrying in the well-used holsters and the man himself who stood so self-assured. Having never seen The Assassin in the shop like Smith had, he had no frame of reference, but felt he looked like a man to be reckoned with.

"Let my son go and I will walk away." said The Assassin. "Pull that trigger and you die."

It was said with such authority, such certainty that a shiver went up Lee's neck. Smith pulled a pistol from his waistband and started to walk forward.

"You little shit," he said but Lee called him back.

"Tell me the whole story and I will think on it," said Lee.

The door suddenly burst open and Surge blundered in and tried to dive across the room to get at Smith. Smith moved like the fighter he was, swinging round on the barely conscious Surge who was moving on will alone and pistol whipped him, knocking him to the floor unconscious. He turned back to The Assassin just in time to see the bullet that went through the centre of his head.

As Surge had attacked, The Assassin had smoothly drawn his pistol from his hip holster, pointed it at Smith and pulled the trigger in one motion. The gun now swivelling towards Lee who just as quick had pulled Jon up in front of him, hugging him close to his body as a human shield.

It was a stalemate and nobody moved. The Assassin had his arm outstretched pointing his gun at Lee and Jon. Lee had his gun in Jon's side holding Jon close.

"Put down your gun," Lee shouted.

"Why?" said the Assassin.

"Because you have no shot," said Lee pressed hard up behind Jon.

"Wrong," said The Assassin and without apparently aiming, pulled the trigger. The bullet sliced along Jon's face leaving a red mark he would carry all his life. It hit Lee in the corner of his eye socket splintering the bone into his eye. Lee screamed and put his hands to his face in agony. The Assassin pulled out the elephant pistol with his left hand, took one step forward and blew Lee's head from his shoulders, the dum dum bullet exploding on impact. He then walked across the room to the already dead Smith, pointed the big gun and fired twice.

Blood and flesh and brains splattered and littered the wall. After the deafening roar of the elephant pistol there was silence and the smell of the gun propellant filled the room. The Assassin stood there for a second then turned and looked first at Surge, who was coming round, and then at The Grey Man.

"Done," he said.

"And done," said Surge.

"And done," said The Grey Man.

The Assassin looked at Jon who was standing shaking where Lee had left him. Blood and tears ran down his face. Collins walked over and hugged his son, kissing the damaged cheek.

"I love you son," he said.

Jon's shaky voice replied. "I love you too dad."

There was a silence. Then Surge said quietly, "Can you please get me to hospital before I bleed to death?"

Chapter 20

The next morning Stevens was sitting in the back of his chauffeured Bentley, soft classical music was playing on the speakers and as always, on his way into work he was reading the Financial Times. His mobile phone rang. He did not recognise the number but decided to take the call anyway.

"Hello," a deep voice said. "Sea here."

Stevens sat bolt upright. "Hello Mr Sea what can I do for you?"

"Nothing," said John Sea. "Thought you might like to hear some news."

"Sure," said Stevens.

"Your friend Mr Peter Lee was involved in an incident last night. They are clearing him up with spoons. Looks like our deal is off."

"A pity," said Stevens.

"Indeed. One more thing," said Sea. "I would take the advice I gave Mr Lee. If you were involved in any way, I would disappear today. I know of these men and trust me they are good, very good."

"Thank you," said Stevens. "But I am only a money man. I have little idea of the day to day issues. I am sure I would be of no interest to these men."

"OK," said Sea. "Your funeral" and rang off.

Stevens thought for a minute then rang the office to talk to Joan his PA.

"Joan how much was in the Peter Lee account?" He waited while she looked it up on the computer.

"Just short of £67 million," she said.

"Thank you, Joan" he said, "I will be in the office in around 20 minutes and will be taking an extended trip. Please book me first class to New York for later today."

"Work?" asked Joan.

"No, pleasure," said Stevens. He hung up and lent back in his seat.

He planned a quick transfer of funds to his offshore account when he arrived at the office. Lee would not need the money and £67 million could pay for a very nice holiday. Whilst he was away he was sure he could find some acquaintances to sort out this trouble. He did know some unscrupulous characters. A smile swept across his face. Looks like everything has turned out well, he thought. Wonder if I have time to visit my club before catching the plane?

He caught the lift to the top floor suite of his offices just off Mayfair. The whole building smelt of money and apart from university he had worked here all his life. Some years ago realising that being crooked was the most fun and quickest way to get rich, he had started to walk on the wild side and now had fingers in so many pies no one quite knew how rich he was, which was how he liked it.

The doors opened and Stevens walked through the open plan office where his accountants had their heads down in their mahogany lined booths then walked through the double doors towards his inner sanctum where Joan should have been sitting. She wasn't. He supposed she was making his morning coffee, very efficient as usual.

He pushed open the door to his office and walked in and was surprised to find two small, old men sitting in his Queen Anne reproduction chairs before his huge walnut and burr desk that had cost a small fortune. He hated anyone in his office alone, far too many secrets. Joan knew this. He looked around at the expensively furnished room and saw everything was in place, his eyes lingering on the Stubbs painting behind which lurked the safe. Everything was as it should be and he relaxed. Both men stood up. They were he guessed mid-sixties but looked quite fit. Both wore business attire, expensive pin stripe suits and handmade shoes. He supposed that's why Joan had let them in. The only jarring item was the man with the swarthy features had on a black cashmere coat that was at least one size too big. But neither looked dangerous. He would have to tell Joan not to do this again. She was getting complacent.

He shut the door and smiled.

"What can I do for you, gentleman?" he said. Suddenly a small gun appeared in the darker man's hand almost by magic, one of those sleight of hand stunts. Stevens looked nonplussed.

"If you fire that I am afraid a number of people will come running," he said.

"I don't think so," said The Assassin. "These walls are soundproofed to cover your little schemes."

"What do you want?" said Stevens.

"You have some money here from one of your clients, a Mr Peter Lee. He will not be needing it anymore and we would like it transferred to a different account."

"I am sorry," said Stevens. "I am not sure if I know that client and certainly do not have the ability to transfer money without specific codes held by my clients."

The Assassin levelled the gun and The Grey Man produced a small pocket recorder. He hit the button and the conversation was replayed between Stevens and his PA, Joan.

"Now," said The Assassin. "We have a couple of ways we can do this. I can start blowing off your feet, then your kneecaps, etc. until you give in, or we can dig out your eye and cut off your fingers to bypass your security on your computer and see what else we can find. What will it be, bearing in mind, Mr Stevens, this is not your money?"

Stevens thought fast. There was a CCTV camera hidden in the room which would identify both men. He was sure he could also put a trace on the money. He just needed to hit one key during the transfer to set off tag software. So why not he thought? Forty eight hours and these idiots would be toast.

He sat at the desk with The Grey Man peering over his shoulder, placed his eye against the eye scanner and ran his forefinger over the fingerprint scanner. The system went on-line and he punched in a code bringing up all the accounts. The Grey Man passed him a piece of paper with a series of numbers. As he finished typing it in, Stevens attempted to hit the tag key but The Grey Man stopped him,

"No, no," he said. "We do not want this traced. Do we?"

"What now?" said Stevens. "You tie me up and leave?"

"I don't think so," said The Assassin and from under his bulky coat he pulled the elephant pistol. "You helped kill my wife," he said.

"No," said Stevens. "I was just the money man."

"That was enough," said The Assassin triggering the powerful gun. Steven's head effectively disappeared, arriving a microsecond later in a pattern of blood and brains covering a large section of the wall, the Stubbs painting, carpet and chair. His headless body stood for a second and then collapsed.

They waited for the echoes of the shot to die away and then opened the door. The soundproofing had been as good as its name and nobody stirred. The Grey Man went behind the desk to see that Joan was still unconscious from the drug he had given her and was out of sight. He switched back on the CCTV camera that filmed Steven's office. They then both walked out as if nothing had happened, two more businessmen in a city of businessmen.

Chapter 21

Surge woke up and looked around. The light filtered in through the Venetian blind showing a wet overcast day. The hospital room was very smart, with its own TV and bathroom, obviously a private room. He had been here for three weeks and he could feel his body healing. The hole from the bullet was stitched and plugged. Luckily it had missed a major artery. There had been no fuss from the hospital, admitting a man with a bullet wound was normally an automatic line to the police. Surge assumed The Firm as usual were involved. His ribs ached but had started to knit as had the bones in his broken cheekbones and the swelling in his face was much reduced. The rest of his body was purple from the bruising, some muscles turning a sickly yellow colour. He had not heard from The Grey Man or Collins, not a note, not a visit. He didn't mind. The job was over. No point crowing about it.

The nurse came into the room. She was a chatty, middle aged black woman who had taken a shine to him. Bustling about she checked his drip that went into his arm and then took his temperature, straightened his pillows and said,

"I have got some good news for you. The doctor feels within 4-5 days, a week tops, you can go home. How about that?"

"Thanks," said Surge with an awkward smile. She smiled back, as she left.

He waited for a few minutes, then with a grunt swung his legs around so he was sitting on the corner of the bed. He carefully pulled out the needle in his arm and detached the drip, then limped over to the closet. Inside was a clean set of clothes from the flat. Jeans, shirt, jumper, shoes and a black long mackintosh with a high collar. He assumed The Grey Man had sent them over. In a drawer was a wallet with a number of £20 notes in a brown envelope. He dressed slowly, then grabbed the walking stick they had given him to allow him to go to the bathroom unaided. As he moved forward he felt something in the mackintosh pocket. He pulled it out and saw it was a letter with Collins neat handwriting on the front. He stuffed it back in and then carefully looked through the glass to see no one was about and hobbled out the door. Turning left through some swing doors, he eased himself painfully down a flight of stairs to the next level, then walked to the lift which he took to the ground floor. Walking slowly but upright he went through reception looking neither right nor left to the taxi rank where he took a taxi to London Bridge and caught the next train home.

He found himself a seat in a section empty of people. He sat at the window watching the rain washing rivulets of dirt down the pane as the train chugged along. The outskirts of London looked as always dirty and faded. He opened the letter from Collins. It read:

Dear Surge

We buried Pru today in a small church in a little village near where she was brought up. Jon and I attended and both Pru's mother and sister were there with a few of Pru's friends. Everyone made a point of telling me what a lovely person she was and she sounded very special. The ceremony was brief and poignant. We laid her in a sheltered grave at the edge of the graveyard near an old elm tree. It is a lovely spot, and the fresh smell of the sea is everywhere.

I cannot tell you how sorry I am that she died Surge and I morn for your loss.

Your dear friend,

Collins

He thought then of Pru and a wave of emotion threatened to overcome him and he steeled himself, letting the thoughts come. He made himself think of all that had happened and all that might have been. His face turned red, his throat choked and tears started to run down his face mirroring the rain on the window pane. He thought of children and the simple things that give most people so much pleasure, holding hands, birthdays and Christmas, but most of all the idea of having a partner to walk through life with rather than continue his loneliness.

Once his mind was full and he could take no more he slammed it shut sealing off the memory and closing down the 'what if's' cauterizing the wound, burning out the softness and becoming again the hard man he had been all his life. At some time in the future he may go there again but he would not let grief take him over.

At his stop he got off and walked slowly through the village leaning heavily on the cane, the rain running through his hair and down his face making his stitches burn. At the door of his small terraced house he searched for the emergency key which he had placed under a stone and let himself in. The house smelt of dust and cold. He lit the boiler and went to his chair in the dining room where, overcome by his efforts, he slept for a few hours. He awoke as the sun was setting and looked around. The small room was lined on every side by shelves and shelves of books. Every scrap of space was taken. His chair was the only piece of furniture placed right in the centre. He sat for a while lost in thought, then stood up having come to a decision. He grabbed a book seemingly at random from a middle shelf, picked up the cane and the still wet coat and went out.

He hobbled along the narrow road smelling the countryside and finally stopped just before the pub where it had all started. The rain was now getting heavier with the wind whipping up and he looked through the window at the same barman standing cleaning what looked to be the same glass. He remembered his dramatic exit, wondered what he might say to stop himself from being barred. Finally he steeled himself and pushed through the front door. The place looked empty. Good, thought Surge, Hate to eat humble pie in public. But astonishingly the barman smiled.

"Lovely to see you sir," he said, "Is it the usual?"

Surge was dumfounded. Then from behind a pillar stepped Collins.

"How did you manage this miracle?" said a shocked Surge.

"Had to buy the pub," he said and with that threw a set of keys at Surge. "Looks like the drinks are on you, landlord."

Surge caught the keys awkwardly and tried to smile but his face hurt too much. The two men walked towards each other and embraced like the brothers they were, before turning towards the bar.

Outside, across from the pub, in the dark and the wind and the rain, if anyone had been looking, they would have seen a small shadow detach from a larger one and start to move away. Anyone looking closer would have seen it was a little old man ambling along, head down moving at a hell of a lick. He appeared to be playing a game with the shadows and the street lights of 'now you see me, now you don't'. If anyone had been asked to describe him they would have struggled. 'Ordinary' they would have said. 'Non- descript. You know, a kind of Grey Man.'

The End

BOOK 2
To Kill a Grey Man
By
D C Stansfield

"Question," said The Grey Man to The Assassin. "How do you kill a man who hides in a crowd?"

"Answer," said The Assassin "**Kill the crowd.**"

The Grey Man is a legend in the covert world of espionage. He has complete control over the powerful organisation called 'The Firm' which supplies the infrastructure for all the Secret Service departments across Europe. Sir Thomas Robertson, "C", head of MI6 wants that control for himself.

The findings of a routine medical show The Grey Man is going blind. Sir Thomas realises this is the break he needs and decides to have him murdered.

However, it is not as simple as killing one old, blind man. The Grey Man has two friends, who he has worked with for decades and are the best in the business. One an assassin, who has been dealing death for nearly thirty years and the other a breaker of men, nicknamed the Surgeon, so vicious, it is rumoured every time he hits a man he cuts him.

Taking no chances, Sir Thomas calls on all his resources including the shadowy figure of John Sea who runs a large part of the UK underworld. "I want them all dead" he declares.

So begins a life and death chase across the South of England.

Can these three men on the verge of retirement take on The Underworld, The Firm and the Secret Service?

What is understood by all, is that this is a game for high stakes and people are going to die!